Welcome to the Secret W

I thought helping Robyn with vice would be a breeze, no way to make some extra cas up being more than I'd bargained for when pets suddenly started disappearing. Turns out they're being snatched! And these crooks aren't just monkeying around—now they've got Oscar, the GC-161 chimp. I've got to get him back before he gives himself—and *me*—away! Let me explain. . . .

I'm Alex Mack. I was just another average kid until my first day of junior high.

One minute I'm walking home from school—the next there's a *crush!* A truck from the Paradise Val ley Chemical plant overturns in front of me, and I'm drenched in some weird chemical.

And since then—well, nothing's been the same. I can move objects with my mind, shoot electrical charges through my fingertips, and morph into a liquid shape . . . which is handy when I get into a tight spot!

My best friend, Ray, thinks it's cool—and my sister, Annie, thinks I'm a science project.

They're the only two people who know about my new powers. I can't let anyone else find out—not even my parents—because I know the chemical plant wants to find me and turn me into some experiment.

But you know something? I guess I'm not so average anymore!

The Secret World of Alex Mack™

Alex, You're Glowing!
Bet You Can't!
Bad News Babysitting!
Witch Hunt!
Mistaken Identity!
Cleanup Catastrophe!
Take a Hike!
Go for the Gold!
Poison in Paradise!
Zappy Holidays! (Super Edition)
Junkyard Jitters!
Frozen Stiff!
I Spy!
High Flyer!
Milady Alex!
Father-Daughter Disaster!
Bonjour, Alex!
Close Encounters!
Hocus Pocus!
Halloween Invaders!
Truth Trap!
New Year's Revolution! (Super Edition)
Lost in Vegas!
Computer Crunch!
In Hot Pursuit!
Canine Caper!

Available from MINSTREL Books

NICKELODEON®

the secret world of

ALEX MACK™

Canine Caper!

Diana G. Gallagher

A MINSTREL® BOOK

Published by POCKET BOOKS
New York   London   Toronto   Sydney   Tokyo   Singapore

This book is a work of fiction. Names, characters, places and
incidents are products of the author's imagination or are used
fictitiously. Any resemblance to actual events or locales or per-
sons, living or dead, is entirely coincidental.

A MINSTREL PAPERBACK *Original*

 A Minstrel Book published by
POCKET BOOKS, a division of Simon & Schuster Inc.
1230 Avenue of the Americas, New York, NY 10020

Copyright © 1998 by Viacom International Inc., and RHI Enter-
tainment, Inc. All rights reserved. Based on the Nickelodeon
series entitled "The Secret World of Alex Mack."

ISBN: 0-671-00690-8

First Minstrel Books printing April 1998

10 9 8 7 6 5 4 3 2 1

NICKELODEON, The Secret World of Alex Mack, and all related
titles, logos and characters are trademarks of Viacom International, Inc.

A MINSTREL BOOK and colophon are registered trademarks of
Simon & Schuster Inc.

Cover photography by Pat Hill Studio

Dog photo by Robert and Eunice Pearcy/Animals Animals

Printed in the U.S.A.

For my mother,
Beryl M. Turner,
in fond memory of her best friend,
Dusty
1988–1996
and for Baron, who shared her grief,
1983–1997
and with affection for Tiger,
who makes her laugh

Canine Caper!

CHAPTER 1

"What's the name of dog number two?" Pausing
at the base of the Mallorys' porch steps, Alex
looked at Robyn expectantly, then glanced at the
tiny Chihuahua at her feet. Growling softly,
Tawney strained against her leash with every
muscle tense.

"Falcon. He's a Great Pyrenees." Pushing her
red hair behind her ear, Robyn glanced at Alex's
pad. "I take him out Tuesdays and Thursdays
after school and Saturday mornings."

Holding the looped end of the Chihuahua's
leash and the pad in her left hand, Alex finished
writing the client's name and address with her
right while Robyn went to the front door. She

had volunteered to take over the dog-walking service for a few days so Robyn could attend a family reunion in two weeks. However, the business had become so successful, taking notes to keep track of everything was an absolute necessity.

"Hi, Robyn!" A smiling woman opened the door, then wiped her wet hands on a flour-covered apron. "Falcon's been sitting here waiting—"

The tense, fawn-colored Chihuahua suddenly flew into a snarling, yapping frenzy as a huge white dog pushed past the woman onto the porch. "Arf! Grrrr—arf! Arf, arf, arf!"

Surprised by the unexpected, ferocious fit, Alex dropped her pad and pen and almost lost her grip on the leash when Tawney lunged. Clinging to the leather lead with both hands, she stared at Falcon in mute shock. He was so big his *head* probably weighed ten times as much as the attacking Chihuahua.

"Quiet, Tawney!" Robyn snapped, as she took the end of Falcon's leash out of his massive mouth.

Sitting down, Tawney grumbled with a throaty growl.

Falcon ignored her foolhardy, canine challenge. Bushy tail wagging in eager anticipation, he was totally focused on Robyn.

Mrs. Mallory shook her head and sighed. "They've been going for walks together for almost a year! Do you think Tawney will *ever* learn to like Falcon?"

"Oh, I think she likes him just fine. She just wants to make sure he doesn't forget who's boss." Smiling, Robyn scratched the big white dog behind his flopped-over ears. "Fortunately, Falcon doesn't care if Tawney *thinks* she is."

Thank goodness, Alex thought as she picked up her pen and pad and added to her notes. The last thing she wanted to report when Robyn returned from her weekend vacation was that Falcon the Congenial had finally lost patience and devoured Tawney the Terrible as an afternoon snack.

Hackles raised, Tawney got in one last bark as an eager Falcon surged forward, pulling Robyn toward the sidewalk.

Catching up, Alex sighed with relief as the little dog settled down and trotted to keep pace with her larger companion. "Why would Tawney try to pick a fight with a dog that's so much bigger than her?"

"I'm just guessing, of course, but I don't think she was looking for a fight. I'm pretty sure it's got something to do with establishing her position in the pack." A delighted grin brightened Robyn's face. "Or maybe because Chihuahuas were bred to flush bears out of caves."

"No way!" Alex laughed.

"That's what someone told me." Robyn shrugged. "I don't know if it's true or not, but whenever I think about a dozen little dogs snarling and snapping at a bear's heels like Tawney just did with Falcon, I'm positive a bear wouldn't hesitate to leave home to get away from the annoying little monsters."

With that image in mind, Alex had to concede the point. "Yeah. I think I would, too."

"And you wouldn't believe how fast Tawney can run!" Robyn rolled her eyes. "She got away from me once when she took off after a guy whizzing by on a bike in the park. Lucky for me Chihuahuas have short attention spans. If Tawney hadn't gotten distracted by a squirrel that ran up a tree, I might never have caught her. Falcon's just the opposite."

"How so?" Alex asked with genuine curiosity.

"The Great Pyrenees were bred to guard sheep from wolves in the mountains, so they have to pay *strict* attention to what they're doing. *Nothing* distracts them from their duty."

"That makes sense." Alex paused thoughtfully, then added, "But if Falcon's a guard dog, why didn't he defend himself against Tawney?"

Robyn giggled. "Well, for one thing, Tawney isn't exactly a threat to his health."

"Not hardly." Alex cast an amused glance at the tiny dog trotting boldly down the sidewalk who was totally convinced she was the toughest thing on four legs.

"And for another, Falcon is one of the most patient, quiet, and gentle dogs I've ever met. All the Great Pyrenees are—unless someone or something threatens whoever they're guarding."

Overwhelmed by how much she had to learn about Robyn's clients and routine, Alex just nodded. She hadn't realized that dogs were such distinctive individuals with just as many different attitudes and personalities as people. Or that she'd have to figure out how to interpret what a particular dog was thinking and saying based on that dog's unique nature and perceptions.

"With school and everything, when did you ever find time to learn so much about dogs, Robyn?"

"I didn't do it all at once. Every time I got a new customer with a different kind of dog, I just looked up the breed in my dog book." Robyn's eyes narrowed slightly. "But you know what's really strange?"

"What?"

"It is *totally* weird how people seem to get dogs that are just like them. You saw how hyper and nervous Mr. Grant was when we picked up Tawney."

"Yeah! And he almost barked your head off 'cause we were five minutes late!" Alex grinned. "Mrs. Mallory seems just as calm and friendly and easygoing as Falcon, too."

"She is," Robyn agreed. "Sometimes I wonder what kind of dog I'd end up with—if I ever got my own dog."

"Why haven't you?" Alex asked.

"Just haven't met the right dog, I guess."

Sighing, Alex lapsed into a pensive silence. She had never thought about getting the *right* dog. She just wanted a dog. *Any* dog. But her mother wouldn't even consider it because she had let the litter box get stinky when they had had a kitten for a few weeks when she was twelve. Although she had been keeping her room clean and doing her household chores without being reminded to prove she was ready for the responsibility of having a pet, her hopes of getting a dog were still pretty remote. Her father was allergic to them.

"That's our next stop." Robyn pointed to a barn-red house with a white picket fence and frowned. "That's funny."

"What is?" Alex didn't notice anything unusual or comical about the quaint bungalow with its carefully tended flower garden, trimmed trees, and freshly mowed lawn.

"Ticket's usually waiting by the gate."

"Ticket? That's an odd name for a dog."

Robyn smiled. "Ms. Huntington made the mistake of going into the pet shop when she was shopping for Florida vacation clothes at the mall a few years ago. She met the perfect puppy and bought *him* instead of a plane ticket."

Alex raised a skeptical eyebrow. "How did she know he was the perfect puppy?"

"She just did. Every dog person I've ever met says the same thing. They just knew their dog was the right dog the instant they saw them."

Alex locked that bit of information away for future reference. Surely her parents wouldn't refuse to let her keep the *right* dog—if she ever found the right dog.

Robyn's frown deepened as she opened the white picket gate. "I hope Ticket's not sick."

"Maybe Ms. Huntington just forgot to let him out." Alex tightened her grip on Tawney's leash as they headed up the stone walkway.

"I doubt it." Shaking her head, Robyn latched the gate behind them. "She works the graveyard shift at The Coffee Café until eight every morning and watches a soap called 'Suburban Shadows' when she wakes up at three. I *always* get here between five and ten minutes after four. The minute Ticket hears the show's closing theme, he starts barking and won't stop until she lets him out to wait for me."

"You're kidding, right?"

"Not at all. He's a poodle and they're incredibly smart."

Keeping a watchful eye on the Chihuahua, Alex pulled her pen and pad out of her pocket. "So you take Ticket every day?"

"Mondays through Fridays except when it rains." Robyn rang the bell and tapped her foot with worried impatience until a young woman wearing a waitress's uniform came to the door.

Falcon whined and Alex noticed that even Tawney seemed unusually subdued. The little dog's brow was actually wrinkled with worry. Given the stricken expression on the young

8

woman's face, maybe the dogs had good reason to be concerned.

"Ticket won't be going for walks with you anymore, Robyn."

"Oh." Robyn tried to hide her disappointed surprise. "Are you working the swing shift at The Coffee Café instead of going in at midnight now?"

Ms. Huntington nodded and Robyn jumped on the opening.

"Well, that's not a problem. I mean, I could still walk Ticket and then lock him back in the house, if you want."

"No, it's not permanent. I'm, uh—just picking up a few extra hours for a while." Ms. Huntington wiped a tear from the corner of her eye.

"Oh, no!" Robyn gasped. "What happened? He didn't—"

Alex didn't even know Ticket, but she gasped, too, in sympathy for the poor woman's loss. But they had apparently jumped to the wrong conclusion about the poodle's demise.

"No!" Ms. Huntington frantically shook her head. "No, nothing like that. Ticket just—doesn't like going for walks anymore. Here's what I owe you." Shoving a check at Robyn, the distraught woman hurried back inside and slammed the door.

Stunned, Robyn stared at the check, then at the door. "I must have done *something* to upset her, but I can't imagine what."

"Not necessarily." Knowing that Robyn always imagined the worst, Alex tried to ease her friend's misplaced guilt by offering the first possible explanation that popped into her head. "She's working extra hours, so maybe an unexpected financial problem has come up. If Ms. Huntington can't afford your service, she might be too embarrassed to tell you."

"Maybe, but she's the second customer I've lost this week." Stuffing the check into her pocket, Robyn shrugged and turned to leave. She had to drag a reluctant Falcon off the stoop, which wasn't easy considering that he outweighed her by thirty pounds.

"What was the problem with the other person?"

"Tuesday, Mr. Constantine said Baron was at the vet's. Then yesterday he called to tell me *he* couldn't afford it anymore. He's retired, but I happen to know he lives very comfortably off his investments and I don't charge *that* much. I just don't understand it." Robyn's frown deepened as she coaxed Falcon down the walk to the gate. Back on the sidewalk, the big dog quickly settled back into his long and leisurely stride.

Alex let Tawney rush forward to catch up. "Well, whatever their reasons, I'm sure it wasn't because they were unhappy with your service."

"Maybe," Robyn fumed, "but there's something else about Ticket that's really bugging me."

"What?" Alex asked with a hint of exasperation.

"Why didn't we hear him barking in the house? Whenever I get here before 'Suburban Shadows' ends, he starts carrying on the minute he hears my voice."

Alex didn't have a clue, but she couldn't face spending a whole afternoon with Robyn fretting over something she couldn't do anything about. "Maybe he's depressed because he *knows* he's not going with you anymore." That didn't seem likely, but it was the only reason she could think of on the spur of the moment.

"You may be right." Pulling Falcon away from a neighbor's mailbox, Robyn sighed. "Dogs have an uncanny way of knowing when something's wrong. Still—"

"So who's next?" Alex quickly changed the subject.

"Tiger Sands. I'll let you take him and Tawney so you can get some practice using both hands."

"Good idea." Alex was amazed at how easily Robyn managed to walk four and sometimes five dogs at one time. She didn't mention it for fear of reminding her that one of the regular Thursday afternoon crowd was absent. "What's Tiger's schedule? Anything special about him that I should know?"

"I'll say!" A mischievous sparkle replaced the somber worry in Robyn's blue eyes.

The somber worry settled over Alex. "Does he bite? Jump on people and knock them down, or what?"

"No. Tiger's a darling little black-and-white Shih Tzu, but—" Robyn fixed Alex with a pointed gaze. "Whatever you do, do *not* let him go anywhere near water. No fountains, no puddles, no kiddie pools, or anything."

"Not even if he's thirsty? Why not?"

"Because Tiger loves to play in water. I learned *that* the hard way. I walked him by an upside-down garbage can lid that was half-full of rainwater and the next thing I knew, he was lying in it." Robyn laughed out loud. "He was dripping wet *and* muddy when I got him home and I promised Mrs. Sands I'd never let it happen again."

"Gotcha." Smiling, Alex made a note.

After they picked up Tiger, Alex tucked her pad and pen into her back pocket and relaxed to enjoy the outing. Walking briskly along the park trails, she had a few harrowing moments when Tawney snarled at passing dogs or snapped to warn the much younger and more rambunctious Shih Tzu to keep his distance. Undaunted, Tiger sniffed, lunged at butterflies, and proudly carried an assortment of sticks he had captured along the route. Falcon walked sedately by Robyn's side, maintaining the quiet dignity and ever-watchful composure inherent to his breed. By the time they headed back to the street to take everyone home, Alex felt more confident about being able to handle Robyn's canine clients for a few days.

"I'm sure you'll do just fine, Alex." Taking the lead down the sidewalk, Robyn glanced back over her shoulder. "And you won't have to look in on Dave's chimp, either."

"*Dave's* chimp?"

Robyn stopped dead and turned, her pale face even whiter than usual. "Oh, gosh. I'm not supposed to tell *anyone* Dave has a chimpanzee! He's afraid his landlady will either make him get rid of Oscar or throw them both out."

Alex started. *Dave?* She hadn't known that the chimp was living with the only person who might be able to identify her as the GC-161 kid.

She had first met Oscar right after he had become exposed to GC-161 one Christmas. Several months later she had found him roaming alone in the park and discovered that he had all the same powers she did. When Vince captured the chimp and took him to Danielle to be dissected, they had both morphed to escape the plant. After that, it was too dangerous to keep him in town where he might be seen, so she had left him at Chappy's old shack in the woods. Dave had obviously found him and taken him home.

"The only reason *I* know," Robyn explained, "is because Dave needs someone to check on Oscar whenever he makes out-of-town deliveries for the plant. He hired me because of my dog-walking business. You won't say anything, will you?"

"Not a word," Alex promised solemnly. She was pretty sure the PVC truck driver wasn't worried about his landlady finding out about Oscar. He just didn't want Danielle Atron or Vince to know.

"Good," Robyn said, looking relieved. "I've been afraid Louis would blab to everyone."

"Louis knows, too?" Alex's eyes widened with anxious surprise. Louis had been so taken with Oscar when she was hiding him at her house, he had offered to buy him. She knew the outspoken boy wouldn't deliberately say or do anything to endanger the friendly chimp, but sometimes Louis just didn't know when to keep his mouth shut.

"Louis saw me trying to catch Oscar one day when he got out of Dave's house. I *still* haven't figured out how he did it. All the windows and doors were locked." Puzzled, Robyn shook her head. "Anyway, Louis offered to substitute for me whenever I couldn't make it. Dave swore both of us to absolute secrecy and, as hard as it is to believe, Louis hasn't said a word."

Alex just nodded as other, more disturbing implications of her friends' association with the chimp flashed through her mind. Oscar's secret was her secret, too. Robyn didn't seem to know there was anything unusual about the chimp— like his ability to morph or zap—but Alex knew from experience that Oscar didn't try to hide his amazing powers. Dave had to know because he lived with the mischievous chimp. Did Louis? If so, she could only hope he realized that Oscar's life would be in danger if the wrong people found out.

Like Danielle Atron. If *she* learned about the chimp's strange abilities, she would escalate her efforts to find the GC-161 accident kid. Alex shuddered and pushed that unnerving prospect to the back of her mind.

"So Dave will call Louis if he needs a chimp-sitter while I'm gone." Robyn resumed walking, quickening her pace as they approached the corner so they wouldn't fall too far behind schedule. "In fact, Louis is going over to Dave's tomorrow—"

Robyn's words were lost in the shrill sound of a surprised human shriek and a screeching feline yowl.

Startled, Alex glanced down the adjacent street to see a man wearing heavy leather gloves struggling with a spitting, clawing, outraged cat. A second man opened the door of a cage in the back of a black mini-van.

A dog in another wire cage began to bark furiously.

Within a split second everything turned into canine chaos.

CHAPTER 2

Alex froze, startled and uncertain about whether to help the cat in distress. Robyn hesitated, too.

The dogs, on the other hand, didn't pause to think. They took loud and immediate action.

Instinctively protective, Falcon perceived a potential threat. Springing in front of Robyn, he barked a warning.

Tawney and Tiger added their frantic, higher-pitched yapping to Falcon and the caged dog's red alert.

Both men looked back, their eyes widening in alarm when they saw the huge white dog braced to defend his "pack."

Taking advantage of the distraction, the cat

leaped from the tall, thin man's grasp and bolted to freedom across the street.

Unable to resist any opportunity to chase something, Tawney took off after the cat, yanking her leash from Alex's hand.

"Tawney!" Holding on to Tiger, Alex gasped as the little Chihuahua barreled away with astounding speed.

"I'll get her!" Shoving the end of Falcon's leash into Alex's free hand, Robyn ran after Tawney. "Tawney! No! Get back here!"

The cat swerved sharply, heading for the nearest tree.

Tawney matched the cat's move like a guided missile, locked on target.

"Uh-oh!"

Still barking, Falcon lunged.

Tiger ducked between Alex's legs to avoid being trampled.

Clutching the big dog's leash, Alex glanced back at the van. Both men were wearing knit caps, which seemed odd since the sun was shining and the temperature was over eighty degrees.

"I'm outta here!" The first man tossed his gloves into the back of the van and ran for the driver's-side door.

"Right behind you!" The second man, who was short and plump, scrambled to close the back hatch.

Barking and whining, the caged dog inside pawed furiously at the door of the wire cage.

Alex couldn't see the dog very well because of the dark interior, but several other significant facts were instantly crystal clear. The van did not bear any official markings or a license plate that identified it as a city government vehicle and the men weren't wearing Animal Control uniforms. They were also getting ready to flee the scene instead of trying to retrieve the cat or give them a citation because Tawney was loose and totally out of control.

Something was definitely suspicious.

And since the circumstances were questionable, Alex couldn't just stand by and watch the captured dog's desperate and futile attempts to escape without doing something. As the short man started to pull the hatch down, Alex aimed a powerful telekinetic thought, releasing the latch on the cage door and throwing it open. Her breath caught in her throat as a beautiful golden collie tried to exit the cage and was rudely yanked to a stop when his collar snagged on the latch.

The man reached for the cage door.

"Run!" Alex yelled.

Suddenly, the dog threw himself forward, breaking free.

The man stumbled backward as the dog flew by and jumped to the pavement, but he didn't even *try* to catch the escapee. Slamming the hatch closed, he raced for the passenger side as the engine roared to life. The collie ran to the sidewalk and paused when the van took off on squealing tires.

Satisfied that the danger was over, Falcon stopped barking and sat down. Looking slightly bewildered, Tiger crept out from between Alex's feet and flopped down beside him. The cat was nowhere to be seen and Robyn had finally cornered Tawney beside a garage two houses back. Assured that everyone else was accounted for and safe, Alex turned her full attention to the elegant long-haired collie as the dog sniffed the air, then took a few hesitant steps in the opposite direction.

Alex briefly considered trying to stop the dog from running by using telekinesis or penning him in a forcefield. However, since invisible restraints might make the dog totally freak, she decided to try a more ordinary approach. "Wait! It's all right. I won't hurt you."

Instantly responding to the reassuring tone of her voice, the dog stopped, looked back, and whined.

"Stay!" Alex hissed the sharp command to Falcon and Tiger and stepped in front of them. Still holding their leashes in one hand, she held out her other to the uncertain collie. "Come on. It's okay. Come here."

Whining again, the dog looked up and down the street one more time. Then, apparently realizing he was hopelessly lost, he sighed and slowly turned his head to focus on Alex.

Afraid that the slightest gesture might send the collie fleeing down the street, Alex didn't move. Several tense seconds passed before the wary dog walked toward her, then sat just beyond reach of her hand.

Behind her, Falcon whuffed and Tiger growled, warning the stranger not to try anything or else.

"Shhhh." Alex hushed them without taking her eyes off the collie. His ears nervously flicked back and forth as she held his worried gaze. Then an inexplicable but definitive sense of mutual understanding and trust seemed to pass between them. Alex fell instantly and unconditionally in love as the dog whined and shoved his muzzle into her hand.

"Good boy. That's a good dog." Suppressing the rush of excitement that was coursing through her, Alex kept her voice even and low as she gently rubbed his chin. *This* was the right dog. She was absolutely sure of it.

"Did you get their license-plate number?" Robyn called as she ran across the street carrying Tawney.

"The plate number?" Alex blinked. The only thing she had noticed, besides the lack of any identifying words on the mini-van, was that the back windows were tinted. "No. Why?"

"Because those guys were *not* from Animal Control." Robyn's blue eyes flashed with angry indignation. "I think they were trying to *steal* that cat. And that dog, too!"

The little Chihuahua, who had been looking suitably ashamed for running away, finally noticed the new dog and launched into another rapid-fire round of yapping.

Alex gasped, expecting the collie to bolt. However, he just moved closer to her and looked at Robyn and the crazed Chihuahua with unflustered curiosity.

Falcon tensed, but kept quiet.

Tiger jumped back and forth in front of the collie, trying to provoke him into a game of doggie dodge. He gave up with a disappointed whimper when the new dog ignored him.

"Pipe down, Tawney! I mean it!" Robyn ordered sternly.

Tawney whuffed in disgust, barked once, and then sagged in Robyn's arms with a disgruntled sigh.

"What makes you think that cat was being stolen?" Alex asked in alarm.

"Well, for one thing, it definitely eats well on a regular basis."

Alex started. "It was running so fast, how could you possibly tell?"

Robyn grinned in spite of the serious implications of the situation. "Because he was so *fat* he barely made it over a chain-link fence before Tawney caught him!" Shifting Tawney into a more comfortable position in her arms, Robyn gave the collie a critical once-over. "And that dog's too well-fed and groomed to be a homeless stray, either. Somebody takes really good care of him."

Alex just nodded and smiled tightly to hide a profound and disturbing disappointment. It had been totally stupid to get instantly attached to the dog without realizing he probably belonged to someone. However, the intensity of her own feelings made her painfully aware of how desperate and frantic the dog's real owner must be.

"Let's get out of here, okay? I don't think those guys would have run away if they were *supposed* to have that dog. And I don't want to be around if they decide to come back 'cause we might be able to I.D. them or something." Setting Tawney down, Robyn glanced nervously over her shoulder as she hurried back toward the corner.

Alex thought Robyn was worrying in the extreme again, but that wasn't her main concern at the moment. As Falcon and Tiger pulled her after Robyn and the Chihuahua, she looked back, expecting to see the new dog following behind. He was still sitting where they had left him. "Hey, boy! Come on!"

The dog whined like he wanted to obey, but he didn't move.

On a hunch, Alex patted the side of her leg. "Heel!"

Without hesitation, the dog leaped forward and fell into a sedate walk at her side. When she rounded the corner, she saw Robyn waiting in the shade of a tall hedge. Curious, Alex stopped. The dog immediately sat down.

"Whoa!" Robyn whistled in admiration.

Then, Alex ordered him to "stay" and moved a few paces ahead. The collie tensed with his ears perked forward, but he didn't advance until she gave him the command to "heel." As soon as he reached her side, he sat and waited patiently.

"That is totally awesome, Alex. Is he tagged?"

"I don't know." Reaching for the dog's collar, Alex felt for the metal strap-keeper and found a bent and empty hook. "The tag's gone. I bet it came off when he got snagged on the cage and pulled free."

"Too bad." Robyn sighed and sagged. "Guess we don't have any choice except to call Animal Control to pick him up."

"No way!" Alex protested hotly. "I'm not sending him to dog jail!"

"It's not jail," Robyn explained impatiently. "That's the *first* place his owner will call to try and find him."

"But the *second* thing his owner will do is put an ad in the paper," Alex countered stubbornly.

Running way behind schedule now, Robyn moved out at a brisk walk with Tawney trotting in the lead. Alex ordered the collie to heel and kept a tight grip on Tiger and Falcon as they sprang forward. When she came up alongside her, Robyn pressed without giving her a chance to interrupt.

"Yeah, but an ad won't appear until tomorrow morning at the earliest, Alex. And some people won't pay for lost dog ads! They just put up signs and that could take days and even *then* there's a chance you'll never see one. And that's assuming that someone's looking for him."

Alex immediately jumped through the loophole in Robyn's arguments for turning the dog in to the shelter. "And what if no one's looking for him? What then, huh? Then he'll be stuck at the pound and it'll cost more than I've got to get him out."

"He's such a great dog, someone's gotta be looking for him, Alex."

"But you don't *know* that, Robyn."

"You're right. I don't." Taking a deep breath, Robyn grimaced apologetically. "But the problem is—I can't keep him while we're waiting to find out. When I started my dog-walking business, I promised my mom I wouldn't bring any clients home overnight."

"Well, then we don't *have* a problem." Alex grinned. "I'm taking him home."

"Oh." Surprised, Robyn blinked. "Okay, but—what about your dad's allergy? The one time I stopped by with a dog and he answered the door, you said he didn't stop sneezing for hours!"

"Yeah, well—" Alex shrugged. "I didn't say it was the perfect solution."

Sighing, Alex placed her hand on the collie's thick fur. The dog looked up, his brown eyes brimming with total trust. She just couldn't let him down. He deserved something better than a cold, dark pen at the pound while she tried to find his owner.

And if his owner couldn't be found, then he'd need a home.

And by then, she would already have proven to her mother that she was willing and able to take care of a pet.

Leaving Robyn to deliver Falcon and Tawney after they dropped off Tiger, Alex detoured into a mini-mart to stock up on anti-allergy pills for her father.

CHAPTER 3

It was almost six o'clock when Alex got back to her own street and spotted her mom's car in the driveway. Her father wasn't home yet. In spite of his allergies, she didn't think he'd resist if she could convince her mother to let the dog stay. And that probably wouldn't be too hard. The dog was so beautiful and well-behaved, Alex was almost positive her mom wouldn't have the heart to send him to the pound, either. Certainly not when she explained that she was launching an intensive search for his owner. She had even picked up the Paradise Valley Press at the mini-mart to prove it.

But that was the back-up plan.

Although it didn't happen often, her mom had bad days just like everyone else. If this was one of those days, the argument would be over before she had a chance to plead the collie's case. She had to wait for exactly the right moment to introduce the dog, rather than barging into the house with her unexpected canine companion and blindsiding her mom. So until that perfect moment came, she had no choice but to hide him.

The dog followed without being told as Alex detoured into a neighbor's yard two doors down from her house. Pausing by the wooden privacy fence that enclosed their next-door neighbor's backyard, she squatted beside the dog and stroked his silky fur.

"You're not going to understand this, boy, but you've just got to trust me, okay?" Alex wished she knew his name, but she had tried dozens of possibilities and he hadn't reacted to any of them. "I promise, this won't hurt a bit."

Not in the least alarmed, the dog just watched her with bewildered canine curiosity as she tucked the newspaper into the back of her jeans. Then she gave him a huge hug—and morphed.

The process didn't require as much concentration as it had when she had first gotten her powers and the transformation was almost immediate. Before the collie knew what was happening, he was experiencing the same warm tingling in his paws that Alex was feeling in her toes, followed by a rush of heat as their molecular structures dissolved into a silvery puddle. When the shift was complete, Alex elongated into a ribbon and oozed herself and the surprised dog through a knothole in the fence.

The dog gave out a garbled yelp when they slithered over a rock, but he didn't utter a sound as they sped over the rough ground behind a row of hedges.

"Sorry," Alex gurgled, trying to soothe him. "It's okay."

Alex knew from conferring with Annie that when she morphed with someone, her passenger retained a complete sense of physical and mental self. Although a rider couldn't separate from her in the morphed state, that individual experienced everything from their own unique perspective. But unlike Annie and Ray, the dog didn't have a clue about the sudden, and perhaps terrifying, change in his physical state. Now that it was too late, Alex wondered if the experience would be *too* traumatic for him.

What if he went bonkers when they rematerialized again?

Worried, Alex zipped under a loose board in the fence into her own backyard and raced for the side door into the garage. An anxious lump formed in her throat the instant she transformed both of them back to normal.

The dog went limp in her arms.

"Hey, boy. Are you all right?" Shaking him gently, Alex stared into the dazed brown eyes. "Boy?"

The dog stayed drooped for a long, excruciating moment, then shook his head and blinked. Jumping to his feet, he whuffed and wagged his tail.

"Shhhh!" Exhaling with relief, Alex rubbed his head and grinned. However, another urgent problem immediately arose.

She heard her dad's car pull into the driveway.

Opening the garage door, she shooed the dog inside and ducked in after him. Collapsing on the cluttered floor, she tossed the rolled-up newspaper at the kitchen door and giggled as the dog jumped into her lap, almost knocking her over. Then, to her horror, the large front door began to slide upward with a grating groan!

Taken totally by surprise, Alex hesitated. No

one *ever* opened the big door! The garage was so completely jammed with stuff there wasn't room for a car, so what was the point? In fact, her father often joked that they didn't dare open it for fear of causing a stuff avalanche in the driveway.

So why was he opening it now?

Why, Alex realized, was hardly important. Hiding the dog was. And the only sure way to do that was to morph again. However, her hand just missed grabbing his collar as he leaped off her lap and ran under the train table. Scrambling on her hands and knees, Alex started after him.

"Hi, Alex. Lose something?"

"Uh—" Smiling tightly, Alex looked up at her father. His forehead wrinkled as he raised a curious eyebrow. Fisting his car keys, he shoved his hands into his pockets. Desperately hoping the dog would stay out of sight, she nodded and sprang to her feet. "Yeah! I, uh—dropped a quarter, but I can find it later." A cloud of dust billowed off her jeans as she brushed herself off.

Her father sneezed.

"Sorry about that, Dad. Guess the floor really needs sweeping." Alex shifted nervously and nodded again. "Maybe I'll do that. Later. After dinner."

Sneezing again, Mr. Mack cast a skeptical glance around. "That should take all of five minutes. There's not much bare floor space to sweep! Ah——choo!"

"Gosh! Maybe you'd better go back outside until the dust settles," Alex suggested hopefully. She almost gasped aloud when she glanced under the train table. The dog was still underneath it, but he was lying by the left front leg. As long as her father didn't look down—

"Good idea. Funny, though—ah, ah, ah—" Tilting his head back, Mr. Mack closed his eyes to finish the monster sneeze. As he whipped his hand out of his pocket, he flipped the car keys out, too.

In the split second before he recovered and opened his eyes, Alex grabbed him by the arm and telekinetically snagged the keys before they hit the floor. Whisking the keys into her hand, she pushed them back into her father's hand as she turned him toward the open garage door.

"Thanks, Alex." Stepping into the fresh air, Mr. Mack took a deep breath and wiped his eyes, which were starting to water. "I've never had a reaction to dust before."

"You're not catching a cold, are you?" Alex noticed that the car was backed into the driveway and a huge cardboard box was sticking out of the car's trunk. Whatever was in it, her father obviously intended to put it in the garage. She glanced over her shoulder and winced. The dog was sitting in plain view by the table leg, head cocked as he studied their puzzling behavior. Shaking her head, Alex shooed him with a brisk, backhanded wave. To her delight and astonishment, he trotted into the shadows by Annie's lab equipment boxes and flopped down on the floor.

"Sick? I certainly hope not!" Absently putting the keys back into his pocket, Mr. Mack untied the rope holding the trunk lid down. "I finally bought a new gas grill and I can't wait to try it out Sunday afternoon. Maybe we should invite Ray and his dad over."

"Great!" Alex struggled to hide an amused grin. The old grill had burst into flames because grease had built up on the propane lines. Her mom had called 911 before her dad managed to smother the fire, and everyone on the block had turned out to gawk when the fire trucks arrived with sirens blaring. "Just don't forget to attach a tin can to catch the grease."

"Don't worry! I've got a bunch of empties stashed." Tossing the rope aside, Mr. Mack tried to pull the large, heavy carton out of the trunk and gave up with a defeated grunt. "It's really wedged in there."

"Maybe not." Leaning over, Alex tugged on the cardboard corners squashed under the trunk lid. With a concentrated telekinetic assist, the corners finally popped free. "Try it now, Dad."

Five anxious minutes later, the grill box was in the garage and Mr. Mack was inside the house. Pressing the automatic garage door control, Alex heaved a weary sigh as the huge panel descended. The dog whuffed quietly from under the train table.

"Okay. You can come out now." Patting her leg, Alex grinned as the collie bounded over. "That was close. Good thing for us it was so dusty in here or Dad might have suspected—"

Whining excitedly, the dog frantically wagged his tail.

Alex blinked as she quickly reviewed what she had just said. Only one word seemed like an appropriate dog name. "Dusty? Is your name Dusty?"

The dog barked, then barked again.

"No! Shhh! You've got to be quiet!" Keeping her own voice down, Alex put her finger to her lips. But the damage was done. Her mother called from the kitchen.

"Alex? What was that?"

With no time to spare, Alex telekinetically sent the dog sliding across the floor and back into hiding under the train table just as her mom opened the kitchen door.

Pausing in the doorway, Mrs. Mack quickly scanned the garage. "I thought I heard a dog barking in here."

"Yeah?" Alex shrugged. She wasn't about to lie. Having her parents' total trust was too important to throw away, even to protect a wonderful dog like Dusty. However, if she didn't confirm *or* deny having a dog hidden in the garage, her mom might just forget about it.

"Hmmm." Perplexed, Mrs. Mack frowned, then looked back as Mr. Mack wandered into the kitchen.

"Have you seen the newspaper, Barbara?" Mr. Mack stopped talking suddenly and stared at his wife.

"Isn't it on—"

Puzzled, Alex wondered what it was about her mom that had caught her dad's attention, then realized he was staring *past* her mother—not *at* her. Dusty! Panic rose in Alex's throat as the collie trotted to the door, picked up the evening newspaper she had tossed onto the floor, and calmly carried it inside.

"—the coffee table?" Mrs. Mack's words trailed off as her gaze followed the dog.

Alex swallowed but didn't say a word to break the stunned silence. However, Dusty was totally unaware that his dramatic entrance had created a major problem. Padding sedately across the floor, the dog sat in front of George with the newspaper gripped firmly but gently in his mouth.

Dumbfounded, Mr. Mack reacted without thinking and reached for the paper. When he sneezed, Dusty dropped it into his hand and whined sympathetically. "Uh, thanks. I think. Barbara?"

Mrs. Mack turned toward the garage. "Alex?"

"Uh—" Sagging, Alex trudged into the house as her father began to sneeze repeatedly. She pulled the small box of anti-allergy pills out of her pocket and handed it to him as she fell into a kitchen chair.

"I assume you have a good explanation." Mrs. Mack's voice was steady and calm as she went to the sink to get Mr. Mack a glass of water.

Alex's heart sank when she heard that totally

cool, unruffled tone. Her mother was *really* upset. "I know it sounds lame, but the truth is— he followed me home. I'm sure he's just lost and not a stray and I want to try and find his owner. Robyn is probably calling the pound right now to see if anyone reported him missing."

Sitting in another chair, Mr. Mack downed the pills as soon as Mrs. Mack handed him the glass of water.

Sensing the man's distress, but not knowing he was the cause, Dusty laid his muzzle on Mr. Mack's knee.

Clapping her hands in front of her, Mrs. Mack backed up and tried to coax him away. "Hey, dog. Over here."

"That's all right, Barbara. It's not that I don't like dogs. He can't help it if his presence makes me miserable. Can you, fella?" Stifling another sneeze, Mr. Mack patted the dog's head and smiled.

Her father's unexpected gesture and understanding attitude gave Alex a spark of hope. She cast a cautious glance at her mom, whose troubled frown indicated she wasn't going to be won over so easily. "Just pat your leg and say 'heel,' Mom."

Mrs. Mack hesitated, her frown shifting between intense displeasure and curiosity. After a few uncertain seconds, she rolled her eyes in surrender and patted her leg. "Heel."

Dusty was instantly at her side. Tongue lolling from the side of his mouth, he sat down and looked up at her with his big brown eyes, ready and willing to obey her every command.

"Not bad." Giving the dog a tentative pat on the head, Mrs. Mack started toward the table. Dusty rose and walked with her. Surprised, Mrs. Mack stopped. The dog stopped and sat down. "Okay, Alex. Now how do I get rid of him?"

Alex grinned. It had taken her most of the way home to figure that one out. "Dismissed."

After issuing the command, Mrs. Mack joined them at the table. As though sensing she was the hard sell, Dusty curled up at her feet. "All right. He's obviously well-trained—"

"Dusty," Alex said. "I think his name is Dusty."

Dusty barked to confirm it.

Mr. Mack sneezed and rubbed his reddening eyes.

Sighing wearily, Mrs. Mack nodded. "But we can't keep him here until someone claims him. What if it takes a few days? Your father's entire weekend would be ruined."

"Well, let's not base our decision on that." Sniffling, Mr. Mack held back another sneeze. "These pills should kick in any minute. I can stand it for a few days."

Everyone jumped when the phone rang.

"That might be Robyn. Maybe she's already found Dusty's owner." Alex's rising spirits plummeted. Although she honestly wanted to see the dog reunited with his family, she had been hoping to spend a little time with him first.

As Mrs. Mack started to rise, Dusty leaped to his feet and ran to the cordless phone on the counter. He had the receiver gripped in his jaws by the second ring and dropped it into Mrs. Mack's lap on the third.

Both Alex and her father leaned forward with anxious expectation.

"Hello?" Nibbling her lip, Mrs. Mack nodded. "Uh-huh. No, it isn't. I'm sorry." After she pushed the "off" button, she looked up and laughed. "It was a wrong number!"

"Hah!" Grinning, Mr. Mack rubbed Dusty behind the ears.

"So he can stay?" Alex asked.

"Looks like I'm out-voted two-to-one so we might as well make it unanimous." Shaking her head, Mrs. Mack glanced at the phone, then at the dog. "I don't suppose you can cook, too?"

Dusty cocked his head and wagged his tail, pouring on the canine charm.

Alex giggled, but she was also suddenly very painfully aware that the longer Dusty stayed, the harder it would be to say good-bye.

CHAPTER 4

At lunch the next day, Alex hurried to join her friends, who were already seated and digging into their food.

"What took you so long?" Ray finished off his first slice of pizza and prepared to tackle the second.

"Did you call the pound again?" Nicole asked.

"Yeah, but no one's called in a report about Dusty yet. There wasn't an ad in this morning's paper, either." Puzzled, Alex frowned as she popped the tab on a fruit juice can.

"Then how come you don't look happy?" Louis asked. "Considering that Dusty is the only thing you've talked about all day, I had the distinct impression you wanted to keep him."

"I do, but—" Sighing, Alex shrugged. "He's so smart and he does so many cool things, it just seems strange that his owner isn't looking for him."

"I agree." Robyn unwrapped her sandwich and jammed a straw through the hole in her milk carton. "I've heard about dogs that answer phones, but I've never actually met one before."

"My parents were certainly impressed." Alex grinned. "They even sent me over to Ray's to call home just to see if he'd answer again."

"Did he?" Nicole asked.

"Every time. Without fail."

Nicole nodded. "Sounds to me like he's a trained assistance dog. They help people in wheelchairs like seeing-eye dogs help the blind."

"Then why isn't someone looking for him?" Louis paused to let the question sink in, then downed the rest of his milk. "Personally, I think he just likes to answer phones for reasons no human will ever comprehend."

"Maybe something happened to his owner." Ray scowled thoughtfully. "I mean, what if the family moved and couldn't take Dusty with them?"

"Right! So they gave the dog away, but he didn't like his new home, and split." Louis paused, then added, "Or maybe they just dumped him."

"I suppose that *is* possible," Alex agreed cautiously. She didn't dare hope, but if Ray and Louis were right, then Dusty needed another home he *did* like. And he obviously liked living with her. He had been like a furry golden shadow that was permanently attached to her from the moment her parents had agreed to let him stay until she had left for school that morning. She suspected she'd find him lying in the front hall, exactly where she had left him, when she got home.

Even better, Alex thought with an amused smile. It had been less than twenty-four hours and her parents were both hopelessly smitten, too. Her mother had decided it was too hot to leave Dusty in the garage while everyone was gone for the day and had let him stay inside. Her dad had made a special trip to the grocery store for dog food last night and today he was calling his doctor to check into recent medical developments in allergy treatments. If nobody claimed him—

Alex slammed the brakes on that thought.

"Okay. It's entirely possible his owner couldn't keep him, but—" Robyn's narrowed gaze swept the table. "Dumping him just doesn't fit somehow."

"Why not?" Louis asked. "It happens all the time. When things get tough and people can't afford to feed them anymore, dogs get abandoned."

"Even so," Robyn countered patiently, "Dusty's trained to the max, he gets brushed regularly, and he's not starving. I just don't think anyone who took such good care of him would have tossed him out to fend for himself or deliberately turned him over to those creepy guys in the van. Something's fishy."

Alex didn't think he had been dumped, either. Although she had dismissed the significance last night, Dusty had stared at the door in wistful anticipation several times, obviously hoping his owner would walk in. No one who had earned that kind of devotion would have abandoned him.

And Alex was certain Robyn was right about the two men. There *was* something fishy about them. They ran away from two high school girls instead of getting angry because the cat escaped or demanding that they give Dusty back.

Nicole, who had been strangely quiet, finally spoke up. "You know what I think?"

"What?" Ripping the seal off a cheese-and-crackers snack, Alex noticed Nicole's grim expression and shuddered.

"I think it's entirely possible those two guys are stealing people's pets and selling them."

Louis blinked. "Actually, that's not a bad theory."

Robyn blinked, then froze with her sandwich poised before her open mouth.

Alex gasped. "Robyn! You don't think—" Yesterday when Robyn had wondered if the men were stealing Dusty and the cat, they hadn't been thinking about the Paradise Valley pet population as a whole. However, Nicole's way of phrasing it had suddenly thrown new light on the matter.

"What?" Wadding his waste papers into a ball, Ray aimed at a trash container ten feet away and threw. The litter-ball sailed in a graceful arc and hit the opening dead center. "Score!"

"Which doesn't count in lost-and-found dog trivia, Ray." Turning back to Alex, Louis repeated the question. " 'Robyn, you don't think—' What?"

Robyn's gaze fastened on Alex. "Ticket and Baron. Maybe they were stolen!"

"Is everyone missing something here or is it

just me?" Nicole asked with a slight, confused shake of her head.

"No," Louis said. "There are definitely some serious holes in my understanding of this conversation."

"Oh, sorry." Alex quickly filled them in on Robyn's sudden loss of dog-walking customers. "And considering how upset Ms. Huntington was when she was talking about Ticket, I think Nicole may be right."

Robyn nodded. "That would explain why we didn't hear him barking, too. Ticket wasn't there."

"Yeah, but—" Ray scowled. "Why wouldn't she just say her dog was missing instead of making up some lame excuse?"

"Another good point." Giving Ray a thumbs-up, Louis turned to Robyn. "Did you see Mr. Constantine's dog when he fired you?"

"Mr. Lack-of-tact strikes again." Nicole rolled her eyes.

Robyn, Alex noticed, seemed too worried about her canine customers to care about the unintended slur. Louis never meant to be hurtfully blunt. He just didn't mince words.

"Actually, now that you mention it—" Robyn looked up. "I didn't see Baron on Tuesday."

"And—" Alex interjected. "Robyn knows Ticket's habits so well, I think we can safely assume that he *is* missing."

"Okay." Taking a deep breath, Louis slapped his hands on the table. "First things first. Before we can start tracking down a ring of pet thieves, we've got to be *sure* there's something to investigate. Beyond a reasonable doubt, anyway."

"Right!" Nicole's face brightened for the first time since the conversation began. Nothing made her day like a worthy cause that required decisive and immediate action. "Beginning with finding out if Baron is missing, too."

"We can stop by Mr. Constantine's house on the dog-walking rounds today," Alex suggested. She and Robyn had already decided to hang up "Found Dog" signs at the main intersections along the way and at strategic locations in the park. "Maybe you can offer Baron a free farewell walk or something."

"It's worth a shot." Robyn sighed. "If Mr. Constantine hadn't cancelled, today would have been Baron's regular walk day. If he's there, he'll be looking out the front window when we arrive."

"Anything I can do to help?" Ray asked.

"Yeah, there is," Alex said. "You and Louis

and Nicole can hang up signs about Dusty in other parts of town. You might run into some other people whose pets have disappeared recently."

"Sounds like a plan to me." Ray gave Alex a high-five.

"I'm in." Nicole nodded, her dark eyes sparkling with a fierce look of determination. Once she sank her teeth into a campaign to right a wrong, nothing could shake her loose.

Alex grinned. When it came to getting things done in a crisis, she could always count on her friends. They had never let her down before and they wouldn't let her down this time, either.

"Well, I can't." Louis shrugged apologetically.

"Why not?" Nicole asked.

"Can't say. Sorry."

"It's okay, Louis," Alex said, graciously letting him off the hook. The rest of them could easily handle the sign distribution.

"Let's meet at The Half-Life at six-thirty to compare notes," Ray suggested.

Everyone but Louis agreed to be there.

With Tawney the Tiny Tyrant on one side and Dusty walking like a perfect gentleman on the other, Alex followed Robyn and a young black lab called Krissy down the sidewalk.

"I don't think Tawney's feeling well today." Frowning, Alex watched the little Chihuahua with growing concern. Instead of straining at her leash and making sure the whole neighborhood knew she was Top Dog, she was hanging her head and dragging her feet.

"Don't worry. She's not sick." Robyn glanced backward with an amused smile. "She just doesn't want to attract Krissy's attention."

"Why not?" Alex asked, puzzled. "Yesterday she made sure Falcon knew she was in charge."

"Yeah, but Falcon's not particularly energetic. Krissy's young and she wants to play, but she doesn't know her own strength. When Tawney charged Krissy the first time they met, Tawney almost got flattened!"

Alex smiled. "Well, Tawney. You may be suffering from delusions of grandeur, but you're not stupid."

Tawney just sighed and kept a wary eye on Krissy.

"Do you have any idea why Louis couldn't help out today?"

Robyn nodded. "Yeah, but you're the *only* person I can tell. Dave had to make an out-of-town delivery and he won't be back until tomorrow night. So Louis is staying with Oscar."

"Right!" Alex slapped her forehead. "I should have guessed. He's serious about keeping Dave's secret, isn't he?"

"Totally. I had to tell Louis that you know, but he said he trusted you to keep your mouth shut."

Alex laughed. Obviously, Louis remembered how protective she had been when she was hiding Oscar in her house.

"After we drop the dogs off, we'll stop by to see how things are going." Dragging Krissy away from a lamppost that smelled particularly interesting, Robyn grinned. "Oscar can get into more mischief than half-a-dozen human two-year-olds."

"Cool." Alex was delighted at the prospect of seeing the impish chimp again and wondered how he'd get along with Dusty.

Robyn stopped suddenly to stare at a house with a huge bay window. A combination riding lawn mower and garden tractor that looked new was parked by the porch with a "For Sale" sign on the seat. "Baron's not there."

"But he could still be in the house," Alex said.

Robyn nodded and turned into the driveway. "Only one way to find out."

A short, stout, middle-aged man with thinning hair, Mr. Constantine did not look happy to see them when he opened the door. He was abrupt to the point of being rude. "I cancelled your service, Robyn."

"Yes, I know, Mr. Constantine, but I thought I'd stop to introduce Alex." Robyn smiled nervously. "Just in case you change your mind. She's taking over the route for a few days in a couple of weeks."

Without being too obvious, Alex positioned herself so that she could peer into the interior of the house. There was no sign of a large terrier-shepherd, mixed-breed dog. Tawney's quiet demeanor was almost absolute confirmation that Baron was not on the premises.

"Fine," the man said curtly. "I'll call you if I need you."

As he started to close the door, Robyn boldly stuck her foot in it. "And since you've been such a good customer, I'd like to take Baron on a farewell walk today. Free of charge!"

"That's nice, but impossible. He's at the groomer's." The man's tone softened as he swung the door closed. "And I will call you if—if I change my mind."

Robyn waited until they got back to the sidewalk before saying anything. "Would you mind going to Pampered Pets on Fourth to find out if Baron's there or not?"

"Nope. That's a good idea." Handing Tawney's leash to Robyn, Alex grimaced. "You don't think he is, though, do you?"

"No, but Louis was right. We've got to be sure the dogs are missing before we start accusing anyone of stealing them."

"Okay, but—" Alex suddenly thought of another source of information they hadn't considered. "If the dogs *are* being stolen, wouldn't these people have called the police?"

"Gosh, yes!" Robyn's face lit up, then quickly darkened again. "But I don't think I'm up for trying to get information out of the local authorities."

"Maybe we won't have to. Ray's uncle works for the City Planning Department. Maybe he's got a contact at the police station. I'll ask him when we meet at The Half-Life later." Bidding Robyn good-bye, Alex headed toward the center of town.

Pampered Pets was easy to find and Alex had

a cover story worked out before she even walked in the door. A woman with frizzy red hair at the counter began to gush over Dusty the instant she stepped inside.

"Oh, he's a handsome one. Collies are such dears, aren't they? And you obviously take good care of him. Look at how his coat shines!" The woman frowned suddenly. "Are you unhappy with your regular groomer?"

"Uh—no. I was wondering if I could put a 'Found Dog' sign in your window." Alex smiled. "Mr. Constantine suggested it. In fact, I think his dog, Baron, is here right now."

"Baron Constantine?"

Alex nodded and held her breath.

"No, he didn't have an appointment today." The woman flipped through her schedule book. "He was supposed to come in Wednesday, but Mr. Constantine cancelled that morning."

"Oh, my mistake." After placing the sign, Alex rushed back outside and turned toward the park to catch up with Robyn. An overwhelming sense of sadness and empathy for the missing dogs and their owners welled up inside her as she broke into a jog.

So far, the only thing they were *almost* sure of was that the men in the van might have been stealing Dusty and that Ticket and Baron were gone. And for reasons unknown, Ms. Huntington and Mr. Constantine didn't want to talk about it.

Alex couldn't imagine *why* the two men would be stealing pets. As far as she knew, adult dogs and cats weren't valuable to anyone except their owners.

There was, however, one thing she was absolutely sure of.

If the dogs *had* been stolen, nothing would stop her from trying to find them, getting them back, and making sure the thieves were brought to justice for their crime.

CHAPTER 5

Even though Alex wanted to see Oscar again, she wasn't thrilled about going to Dave Watt's trailer. On the rare occasions when she did run into the truck driver who was responsible for dousing her with GC-161, he was always nice. But the possibility that he'd suddenly remember that she was the kid Danielle Atron was looking for was always there, too. She was pretty sure Dave wouldn't knowingly do anything to harm her, but he wasn't exactly the brightest man she had ever met. So for safety's sake, she just avoided him.

But today, Alex reminded herself, as she and Dusty and Robyn turned onto the path leading to the trailer, he was speeding north on the Interstate in a Paradise Valley Chemical truck and she didn't have to worry.

"Uh-oh." Robyn stopped abruptly.

Or did she?

Following Robyn's gaze up the hill, Alex relaxed. Robyn hadn't spotted Dave coming home unexpectedly. Ray and Nicole were pounding one of the "Found Dog" signs into the ground. Nicole waved as Ray gave the sign stake a final *whack*.

"Do you think Louis will believe we ran into them by accident?" Robyn asked.

"Hard to say, but I don't think it's a huge problem. I'm sure we can trust Ray and Nicole to keep Oscar a secret. Ray's met him before and Nicole would rather serve detention for a year than snitch on a helpless animal."

Although, Alex thought, *Oscar is far from being helpless.*

"Oh, I'm sure we can trust them, too. It's just that—I promised, you know?" Robyn slumped with a defeated sigh as Ray and Nicole started toward them.

"Yeah, but it's not like you broke your word on purpose or anything. Besides—" Alex glanced at Dave's trailer, which was situated fifty yards back from the road. "We're not *at* Dave's place. We're just walking down the street. So maybe they won't find out Louis is chimp-sitting."

And they probably wouldn't have, either, Alex reflected as Dave's front door suddenly flew open. Having just reached the edge of Dave's hugh fenced-in yard, Ray and Nicole looked up when Louis appeared in the doorway and yelled.

"Okay! Where are you?"

"Right here!" Ray smiled and waved, then pointed Nicole toward the gate.

"Not you! Oscar!" Although red-faced with fury and frustration, Louis realized his mistake the instant the chimp's name passed his lips.

"Great!" Robyn grinned as she, Alex, and Dusty jogged forward. "Now Louis can't put the blame on me for letting the cat out of the bag."

"Or chimp, as the case may be." Skidding to a stop by the gate, Alex slipped her fingers through Dusty's collar as Louis ran across the yard. Since the dog had probably never met a chimpanzee face-to-face before, she didn't want him to run off if Oscar decided to pop out of the bushes screeching the ape equivalent of "boo!"

"Oscar?" Ray came to a startled stop. "Oscar lives here? With Dave?"

"Who's Oscar?" Nicole asked, without directing the question at anyone in particular.

"Oh, boy." Pausing on the other side of the gate, Louis ran his fingers through his hair and exhaled loudly. "Sorry, Robyn. Guess I really goofed."

"In what way—specifically?" Totally confused, Nicole eyed Louis, then shifted her puzzled gaze to Robyn.

Standing behind Nicole, Ray glanced at Alex and asked for confirmation of Oscar's residence by pretending to scratch under his arms like a monkey, then pointing toward the trailer.

Alex nodded.

"Don't worry about it, Louis," Robyn said. "I'm sure Ray and Nicole won't say a word."

"Well, I can guarantee that *I* won't say anything!" Nicole huffed. "Since I don't have the faintest idea what you're talking about!"

"We're talking about Oscar," Ray said patiently. "He's an ape."

"And Dave's best friend," Robyn added.

"Who got out when my back was turned again!" Shaking his head, Louis scanned the area surrounding the trailer.

"Okay." Calming down, Nicole sighed. "So would someone please explain to me why we *care* that Dave's roommate decided to vacate the premises?"

"It's a long story." Louis opened the gate and motioned them all inside. "Oscar's not exactly an ordinary roommate."

"Shouldn't we be trying to find him?" Alex didn't want to be an alarmist, but the chimp was nowhere in sight. That didn't necessarily mean he wasn't in the yard. Oscar could morph at will just as she could. The little rascal had probably oozed out of the house in liquid form through the dryer vent or under a crack in the door. But she couldn't tell Louis that and he wouldn't believe her anyway.

"He'll show up when he figures out I'm not gonna cooperate. We go through this routine all the time." Louis threw up his hands in exasperation. "He loves to play hide-and-seek and he's extremely good at the hiding part."

No doubt, Alex thought with a wry smile. Oscar the Puddle was probably laughing at them from the mailbox.

"You mean Oscar *really* is an ape?" Nicole started. "Ape like in gorilla?"

"Chimpanzee." Ray grinned.

"But you have to promise not to tell anyone,"

Robyn said pointedly. "Dave doesn't want anyone to find out."

"No one will hear it from me." Intrigued, Nicole stepped off the walk to peer under a leafy, flowering shrub. "Come out, come out, wherever you are!"

"Be careful, Nicole," Louis warned. "I think the underground power lines in this yard are faulty. I'm always getting these weird little shocks."

Nicole immediately let go of the branch she was lifting. "That could be really dangerous. A short could shut down the electricity for miles around."

"I know." Louis shrugged. "I keep telling Dave he should have Paradise Valley Power come check it out, but he won't listen."

Did Dave know Oscar the Mad Zapper was responsible? Alex wondered, then spotted an orange tennis ball lying in the grass.

"Does Oscar play with that ball, Louis?" When Louis nodded, Alex picked it up and held it under Dusty's nose. He wasn't a tracking dog, but she was pretty sure most dogs could recognize individual scents. "Can you find this guy?"

Snorting at the odd odor, Dusty backed off a

step and cocked his head. Then he lowered his nose to the ground.

Ray's gaze skimmed the chain-link fence that enclosed the entire lot. "How can you be so sure he's still in the yard, Louis? Oscar could scale that fence in under a second."

"No reason, except that he always is," Louis said. "Maybe he learned his lesson after he ran off and got lost that time Alex found him."

Barking frantically, Dusty suddenly took off across the lawn toward the backyard.

"Awesome!" Louis grinned. "I think he found him."

Alex bolted after the dog without taking the time to respond. Dusty wasn't barking just to alert her to something he thought she should investigate. He was racing to the rescue.

Ray zoomed past her on his much longer legs and stopped at the overgrown hedge growing along the back portion of the fence.

Dusty was whining and trying to dig his way under it. After a few seconds, he ran barking into the corner.

Peering over the top of the hedge, Ray yelled out just as Alex and the others reached him. "Hey! Stop!"

Standing on their tiptoes, everyone looked to

see who Ray was screaming at. Alex gasped along with everyone else when she saw the tall, thin man and the short, stout man put the limp chimp into the back of the black van. When Ray called, they both began to fumble in panic. The tall man almost slammed the short man's hand in the door as he pulled the hatchback closed.

Ray shoved through the hedge and grabbed the top rail of the fence to vault over it, but Alex knew the effort was in vain. Since the two men obviously preferred to run whenever they were caught in the act, they didn't seem particularly dangerous. But they *had* left the van running so they could make a quick getaway and they had parked too far away for Ray to catch them in time. In her liquid state, she might have been able to reach the van and slither inside before the back hatch closed—except there were too many witnesses and she didn't dare morph!

But there was something else she could try.

Racing to the corner where Dusty was barking, Alex squatted down at the end of the hedge, peered through, and groaned. The license plate was covered with mud. Without some kind of identifying mark, there was no way to distinguish this black mini-van from dozens of others in Paradise Valley!

Desperate as the two men jumped into the front seat, Alex took aim and fired a long-range zapper. The electrical charge hit the right rear corner of the van. The shiny paint sizzled, then cracked and peeled. It wasn't a very big mark, Alex thought as the van sped away, but it was better than nothing.

"The plate number!" Robyn shrieked. "Get the license plate number!"

"Can't." Backing out of the hedge, Ray shook his head. "They were parked too far away."

"It was covered with dirt so you couldn't read the numbers anyway," Alex said as she jogged back.

Pale and shaken, Louis swallowed hard. His eyes had a glassy, dazed look of disbelief. "Don't tell me those guys just stole Oscar."

"Those guys just stole Oscar," Nicole said bluntly.

"I'm afraid they did, Louis." Ray placed a sympathetic hand on Louis's shoulder. "I guess Oscar isn't smart enough to know he shouldn't trust strangers."

"Especially when they tempt him with something a chimp can't resist." Robyn pulled a banana peel out of the hedge. "How much do you want to bet there was a tranquilizer in this?"

Stunned, Alex hugged Dusty when he gave up his futile chase and returned to her side. Then, keeping her hand on his head, she lagged behind as everyone slowly walked back to the front of the trailer. Aside from being worried about Oscar, she was suddenly faced with a potentially disastrous problem.

When the pet thieves found out about Oscar's powers, they'd know that they had stumbled onto something of significant scientific interest and value. Their next step would be to contact the CEO of Paradise Valley Chemical. The plant was the only scientific research and development institution in town and everyone knew that Danielle Atron would buy promising ideas and research developed by junior and amateur scientists.

And Alex was certain Danielle would be more than a little interested in Oscar.

Vince had told her that the chimp had been exposed to GC-161. Even though Oscar had escaped the PVC lab before that could be confirmed, Danielle would not dismiss a second chimp capture as coincidence. Chimpanzees weren't exactly common in Paradise Valley. And once Danielle had him, it wouldn't take long to figure out that the chimp could zap, morph, and use telekinesis.

Then she and Oscar would both be doomed!

Alex shivered, even though the temperature was above eighty degrees.

"How am I going to explain this to Dave? I mean, he was depending on me to take care of Oscar!" Hanging his head, Louis shoved his hands into his pockets and kicked at the grass.

"Well, Dave won't be back until tomorrow night, so maybe you won't have to tell him," Ray said hopefully.

"I think he'll notice that his chimp is missing, don't you, Ray?" Shaking his head, Louis leaned against the trailer door.

"Yeah, but Oscar's got some tricks up his sleeve." Ray looked back at Alex and smiled grimly. Unlike the others, who didn't know about her powers, Ray realized that *her* life was in jeopardy, too. "If we don't find him first, he might escape on his own."

"That's right," Robyn said brightly. "Dave has sealed up every possible escape hatch in this trailer and Oscar's always getting out anyway. I never have been able to figure out how. And neither have you, Louis. So if there's a way to get free, he'll find it. I'm sure of it."

"Maybe," Louis said. "As long as those guys don't *keep* him tranquilized."

Alex stopped dead. The men would never have been able to capture Oscar if the chimp had been conscious. And although the best-case scenario was that Oscar would use his powers to escape when the two men weren't looking, the chimp didn't know he should exercise discretion. Wide-awake and mischievous by nature, he probably wouldn't hesitate to morph in front of witnesses. However, if he was *unconscious*—he *couldn't* use his powers! And if he didn't use them—the men would never find out about them!

There was *no* question that, since Oscar was already a prisoner, they would both be better off if he slept in blissful and powerless oblivion until he was rescued. Although she wasn't positive, Alex was fairly certain the thieves wouldn't have given the chimp anything dangerous. Even without his powers, Oscar was too valuable an animal to risk harming.

"Unfortunately, that's probably what they'll do, Louis." Ray sighed. "Oscar can make an awful lot of noise when he's upset. If it was me, I'd want to keep him sedated—and quiet."

"Exactly," Robyn said. "So shouldn't we be

doing something that might help get him back? Like call the police?"

"An excellent idea." Bounding through the door, Louis led the way to the phone in the kitchen. It rang as he reached for the receiver.

Dusty jumped toward the counter, but Louis picked up first. Dropping back to the floor, the dog laid down with an indignant huff.

"Hello?" Louis frowned. "Who is this?"

Alex exchanged nervous, questioning glances with Robyn, Ray, and Nicole as Louis's mouth fell open and the blood drained from his face.

"I gotta have more time!" Louis practically shouted into the receiver, then nodded, and slowly hung up.

"Who was that?" Nicole asked.

"The pet thieves. Or maybe I should say pet-nappers." Louis's voice cracked and he paused to take a deep breath. "That was the ransom call. They want five hundred dollars by six o'clock tomorrow evening or—"

"Or what?" Alex asked.

"Or we'll never see Oscar again."

CHAPTER 6

In spite of the dismal circumstances, the atmosphere in Dave's trailer was charged with energy. No one, Alex noted with pride, was going to let the magnitude of the problem deter them from trying to solve it.

"Was the caller a man or a woman?" Nicole asked.

"I couldn't tell." Louis sighed. "It was too muffled and kinda whispery. But totally menacing and dead serious."

"So what do we do?" Falling into a metal chair at a cluttered table, Ray dropped his chin on his folded arms and glanced at Alex.

Alex sank into another chair that didn't come close to matching the metal one, and answered with a slight nod. Except for Ray, no one knew that they had a unique advantage over the pet-nappers because of her powers. She intended to put them to good use. "Come on, Dusty. Over here."

Moving to Alex's side, the collie put his head in her lap and gazed at her with troubled eyes.

"Don't look so worried, boy." Alex smiled. "If it wasn't for you, we wouldn't know that Oscar had been stolen."

"That's the truth." Ray leaned over the table. "Good dog."

"I think he's just upset because Louis didn't let him answer the phone," Robyn said.

"He'll get over it." Louis began pacing and gave Dusty a pat on the head as he walked by. "As I see it, we need to get moving on *two* plans."

"Plan number one. Call the police." Robyn reached for the phone.

"No!" Spinning around, Louis jumped back to the counter and put his hand over Robyn's. "We can't call the police."

"Why not?" Nicole frowned. "Stealing Oscar

probably amounts to grand larceny or something."

"Not quite, but that's not the problem." Louis sighed heavily. "The caller said I *definitely* wouldn't see Oscar again if I called the police."

"That explains a lot." Absently scratching Dusty behind the ears, Alex frowned. "Like why Ms. Huntington and Mr. Constantine didn't tell Robyn the real reason they cancelled her dog-walking service. They couldn't take the chance that she'd tell the police."

"And we can't tell *anybody* else, either." Louis's eyes narrowed with warning. "Not even our parents. My dad would be on the phone in thirty seconds flat."

"Mine, too." Robyn nodded, then paused thoughtfully. "I bet Mr. Constantine's trying to sell his new lawn tractor to raise the ransom money."

"Probably," Alex agreed. "And Ms. Huntington's probably working extra hours for the same reason!"

"Except—" Robyn scowled. "Baron's been missing since Tuesday. Almost four days. The pet-nappers must have given Mr. Constantine longer than twenty-four hours to come up with the money. How come they wouldn't give you more time, Louis?"

"They didn't say and I didn't argue."

"Maybe because a chimp isn't as easy to take care of as a dog. I don't think the thieves can buy 'chimp chow' at the local market." Ray shrugged. "What does he eat, anyway?"

"Irrelevant. Why they wouldn't give me more time doesn't matter, either. Either I pay up by six tomorrow and they give him back or—" Running his hand through his curly hair, Louis sagged against the counter. "Or they'll dispose of him elsewhere."

"Dispose!" Nicole stood up. "What did they mean by that?"

"Sell," Alex said quickly. "I'm sure they meant sell. He wouldn't be worth anything if he was, uh—you know."

Except to Danielle Atron, Alex thought, remembering how close the chimp had come to being dissected in the PVC lab. Fortunately for Oscar, the pet-nappers didn't know that. Neither did any of her friends, except Ray, and they didn't need to know. Louis was feeling guilty enough without worrying about the worst that could happen.

"They thought you were Dave, didn't they, Louis?" Robyn asked.

"Yeah, and I didn't want to say I wasn't 'cause I'm hoping we can get Oscar back before Dave gets home tomorrow."

"Which brings us back to my original question," Ray said. "What are we going to do?"

"For one thing, I've got to come up with five hundred dollars." Louis pulled a crumpled wad of bills out of his pocket and counted. "Fourteen. Well, that only leaves four hundred and eighty-six to go."

"That's an awful lot of money, Louis." Ray sighed. "I can only chip in about fifty because I went on a CD-buying binge last weekend."

"I've got forty dollars and some change stashed at home. And this." Robyn pulled three dollars out of her purse and held it out. "My mom makes me put most of my dog-walking money into a savings plan I can't touch."

"Count me in for sixty-three," Alex said. It wasn't much, but it was everything she had.

"Thanks. If I have to, I'll sell my silver coin collection to make up the difference." Louis shrugged. "Or maybe my *dad* would take my stereo as collateral on another loan—"

"Hold it!" Raising her hands, Nicole shook her

head. "I'm sorry, but I'm not sure we should *pay* them anything!"

"Me neither, but it's only as a last resort." Stuffing his bills back into his pocket, Louis waved Robyn's money away. "Just hold onto it until tomorrow. Paying the ransom is Plan B. First, we're gonna try and find those jerks and nail them."

"That's more like it!" Nicole grinned.

"Yeah!" Ray nodded emphatically. "For all we know, they've been running this scam for years and making a small fortune!"

"Maybe not so small," Robyn said. "All my customers would pay to get their dogs back. No questions asked. If those guys only stole and collected on one pet per day, that's thirty-five hundred dollars a week!"

"Tax-free," Nicole added. "And we know they almost snatched *two* animals yesterday. The cat and Dusty."

Alex inhaled sharply, suddenly realizing why Dusty's owner hadn't called the pound or put an ad in the morning paper. Even though Dusty had escaped, the pet-nappers must have called to make a ransom demand anyway!

"These guys have *got* to be stopped." Nicole's

eyes flashed. "But I don't have a clue where to even start looking."

"We just start," Louis said. "If we get going early, the five of us should be able to cover most of Paradise Valley by late afternoon. There's a good chance we'll spot that van."

"I hate to put a damper on this," Robyn said. "But do you have any idea how many black mini-vans there are in this town?"

"A hundred?" Louis winced.

"At least!" Ray rolled his eyes.

"But I bet only one of them has a spot on the right rear corner where the paint is cracked and peeled." Alex grinned. "I saw it when they pulled away."

"And don't forget," Ray added. "Alex and Robyn have seen that van two days in a row."

"Right. . . ." Robyn nodded uncertainly. "So assuming the pet-nappers don't decide to lay low and take the day off tomorrow, what's the plan if we *do* spot it?"

"Try and get the license number and follow it," Louis said matter-of-factly. "They're either holed up nearby or there're three of them."

Ray looked up skeptically. "How do you figure that, Sherlock?"

"Easy." Louis grinned smugly, pleased with

his deductive ability. "Because they called no more than five or six minutes after they drove away. So either there's a third person at the hideout or the two guys got there in five minutes and called."

"Unless they used a cell phone." Robyn shrugged.

"Or a pay phone along the way," Nicole said.

"Okay!" Folding his arms, Louis set his jaw. "If anyone has a better plan, I'm listening."

Alex *did* have a better idea, but she couldn't tell anyone except Ray. However, since no one else had an alternative plan to suggest, Louis's Plan A was a go.

Pulling a stool up to the counter, Louis sat. "If we don't find them by five o'clock, we'll pool our money and pay."

"And as long as we're covering the whole town anyway," Alex added, "let's put up some more signs about Dusty. I'll make as many as I can tonight. Hopefully, his owner will spot one of the signs before paying the ransom."

Robyn nodded. "Especially since the petnappers don't *have* Dusty to give back."

Dusty barked.

"Dusty seconds and the motion carries," Louis said. "We'll distribute more signs."

"Better put a 'found' ad in the Paradise Valley Press, too, Alex," Ray suggested.

"I would, but—what if we need every cent we've got to pay Oscar's ransom?"

"No problem. *Found* pet ads don't cost anything and—" Ray sat back and grinned. "Since it's past the classified deadline for tomorrow night's edition, I'll call Mr. Hardwick and see if he'll make an exception and get it in as a *personal* favor to me."

"Thanks, Ray." Alex didn't know how much pull he had with the editor of the paper he delivered, but she appreciated the offer.

"All right!" Louis clapped his hands together. "We've got a plan! We've got force and motivation. So let's—"

The phone rang.

Everyone froze—except Dusty. Leaping for the counter, he picked the phone up on the second ring, then happily dropped it into Louis's reluctant hand.

"Hello? Oh—uh, hi, Dave!" Wincing, Louis nodded. "Oh, yeah. Everything's fine. Uh-huh. Oscar? Well, he's—uh, hiding! Yeah, well, he'd probably love to say 'hello,' but you *know* he won't come out until he's ready. Yeah. Right. See ya then. Bye." Slamming the receiver down,

Louis collapsed across the counter in a state of breathless anxiety.

"Are you okay?" Nicole asked.

"Just great." Taking a deep breath, Louis straightened and set his jaw with grim resolve. "One way or another, we have *got* to get those crooks."

Absolutely, Alex thought as she began to plot Plan C.

CHAPTER 7

"Looks like you're mounting a major expedition, Alex." Freshly showered and shaved, Mr. Mack stepped off the front porch and bent over to ruffle Dusty's fur when the collie ran over to greet him. "Hey, boy! How ya doing?"

Looking up from the signs she was dividing into five piles, Alex smiled. "That new allergy medicine seems to be working, huh, Dad?"

"Sure does." Breathing in the morning air, Mr. Mack sighed with contentment, then shot Alex a cautionary glance. "But Dr. Lyons did say that it might not be effective over a long period of time because some people build up an immunity."

"But he wasn't sure." Alex desperately hoped her father wasn't one of those people. If the medication worked, her parents would have one less reason to veto having a dog.

Picking up a stick, Mr. Mack tossed it across the yard and grinned as Dusty ran after it. "Come on, guy! Bring it here!"

On the other hand, Alex thought as the collie bounded back and dropped the stick in her dad's hand, if they didn't find Dusty's owner, keeping *him* would *not* be a problem. Allergy or no allergy.

"So where are you off to today?"

"Everyone's coming over to help me put up 'Found Dog' signs." That was only half the truth, but Alex knew her parents would absolutely forbid her to try tracking down a ring of pet-nappers. And Oscar's safety might depend on keeping the police out of the picture. The rescue team would call the authorities after they found where the stolen pets were being kept.

"Breakfast, George!" Mrs. Mack called through the front door, then ran back to the kitchen.

"Coming!" After throwing the stick one more time, Mr. Mack went inside.

Alex's friends all arrived within the next ten minutes, prepared for a long day. Robyn had borrowed her mother's twenty-one-speed mountain bike and Nicole was riding a sleek and faster twenty-one-speed touring bike. Both of them had full water bottles strapped to their bike frames. Mr. Alvarado's binoculars hung around Ray's neck.

"You look terrible, Louis!" Nicole observed bluntly.

"I didn't sleep much last night." Dropping a backpack that was stuffed to the bursting point, Louis yawned. "I kept imagining all kinds of terrible things that could happen to Oscar and then, when I *did* doze off, I dreamed about it!"

"Yeah. It was nightmare city for me, too." The dark circles under Robyn's eyes were accented by her ultra-fair skin.

"But don't worry—" Louis yawned again and shook his head. "I'll rally."

"Good." Alex hadn't actually slept well, either. She was running on raw nerves and willpower, but like the others, her desperate determination to rescue Oscar and all the other animals the pet-nappers had captured made up for the lack of rest. "I think we should split up into teams. That way, one person can follow the van while the other one finds a phone. Except for me and Dusty, of course."

"Not necessary." Opening his backpack, Louis pulled out five military-type walkie-talkies. He held up one and turned it on to demonstrate. "I got these from my dad's inventory. They're supposed to have a range of at least a mile. We won't all be in range of each other all the time, but we can stay in touch if we relay messages from one person to another."

"Cool!" Taking one of the devices, Ray flicked it on and depressed the "talk" button. "Radical Rover to Fearless Fido. Come in. Over."

Dusty's ears perked up when Ray's voice sounded from the walkie-talkie in Louis's hand. Alex grinned. The com-device did resemble a cordless phone receiver.

Louis blinked and answered through the hissing walkie-talkie. "Fearless Fido? I think we should just stick to our real names, don't you, Ray? Over."

"I definitely do," Alex said. "Not that using code-names wouldn't be cool, but it might be too confusing. I mean, we can't take a chance on being misunderstood."

"That's right," Robyn agreed.

"Lives are at stake," Nicole added for good measure.

"Okay. You've got a point." Ray shrugged, then brightened. "But if I *do* use a code-name, then you'll know I blew my cover and the bad guys nabbed me."

"The point is to nab *them*, Ray," Alex said seriously. "So don't do anything heroic, okay?"

"Wouldn't think of it." Noting Alex's skeptical look, Ray held up his right hand. "Promise. If I see the van, I'll call and wait for back-up. I just want to find Oscar and get the evidence to put those guys away."

Nodding, Alex relaxed. The team was in unanimous agreement on the mission's objective.

After giving signs to everyone, Alex checked her own backpack to make sure her water bottles weren't leaking and turning Dusty's dog biscuits into a soggy mess. She also had a small hammer, nails, a small dish for Dusty's water, and a variety of granola bars.

Louis handed out the walkie-talkies and mounted his bike. "Everyone knows their territory. Just check in every now and then so we don't lose track of each other."

"And we're supposed to meet back at Dave's trailer by five, right, Louis?" Ray asked.

"Affirmative. Unless we find that van. If we don't, the pet-nappers are going to call at five-thirty to tell me where to take the money."

Since Alex was walking, she and Dusty had been given the area closest to the Mack house. As she started out, she really didn't think she had much chance of spotting the pet-nappers' van. However, five blocks and an hour later, she caught a glimpse of a black mini-van in a garage.

A tall, thin man stepped out of the shadows, looked up and down the street, then activated the garage-door mechanism.

Alex froze as the door slid down. The man's actions seemed suspicious and one of the pet-nappers was tall and thin. Beyond that, she couldn't tell if there was any resemblance. Although she and Robyn had seen the men twice, things had happened too fast and she had been too far away to get a good look at their faces. Oddly enough, that was probably why Dave hadn't been able to identify her after the GC-161 accident, either. It had happened too fast and she had been covered in gold gunk.

That, however, was totally irrelevant to the problem at hand.

"I think we gotta go for it, Dusty."

Since he didn't have a clue what she was talking about, the dog just cocked his head and wagged his tail.

With the collie at her side, Alex ducked behind a short hedge that formed a border between the mini-van house and the neighbor's. She wasn't going to call for help until she knew she had the right van. Besides, she had some highly efficient surveillance techniques that weren't available to her friends. Squatting down and throwing her arms around the dog, she morphed.

Relieved because Dusty didn't show any signs of being upset this time, Alex slithered to the side door and oozed under it into the dimly lit garage—right in front of the man's feet.

"Ow!" Alex yelped, reacting instinctively when the man, who was carrying a large bag of lawn fertilizer, stepped on her. Zipping under the car, she huddled in quivering panic.

"Wha—" The surprised man stumbled, dropping the bag and barely keeping his balance. "Who's there?"

"Arf!"

Dusty's gurgled bark alerted the man to their position. As he fell to his hands and knees to look under the van, Alex slid to the rear and puddled behind the right rear tire.

"Here, doggie. Where are you?" Standing up, the man moved to the front of the van. "Come on out."

Alex moved toward the closed front door and looked up.

The black paint on the right rear corner of the mini-van was shiny and smooth.

"Arf! Arf!"

"It's okay, guy," the man said softly. "How come you sound like you're under water?"

Slithering back to the outside wall, Alex headed toward the side door as the man worked his way down the other side of the van. As she oozed back outside, she heard the man call his wife.

"Hey, Alice! You're not gonna believe this, but I think our garage is haunted by a dog ghost that drowned!"

Materializing by the hedge, Alex looked at Dusty sternly. "Don't you know you're supposed to be *quiet* when you're engaged in undercover operations?"

Looking quite pleased with himself, Dusty licked her cheek.

"Well, it's my fault for being in such a hurry

to check out that van. Next time, remind me to look before I slither, okay?"

"Arf!"

"There!" The man's voice carried from the garage. "Hear that?"

The large garage door opened as Alex hit the sidewalk with Dusty at her side. She heard a woman laugh.

"I think your ghost is walking down the street, dear."

Smiling, Alex wondered how the rest of the team was making out and decided to check in. Unclipping the walkie-talkie from the waistband of her jeans, she made contact with Robyn. Fascinated with the "talking" phone, Dusty cocked his head and listened with acute canine interest.

"Can't talk now, Alex," Robyn said anxiously. "I've got a possible match at the Hayes Avenue Shopping Center. Over and out."

Stuffing the walkie-talkie into her bag and gripping Falcon's leash, Robyn cautiously approached the black mini-van parked at Super Foods. She was sure she had heard a small dog barking inside it.

Having Falcon with her made her feel just a little bit more secure. Since it was his normally scheduled walk day, she had picked him up as usual. Mrs. Mallory had been delighted when she offered to watch him all day at no additional charge. As she crossed the pavement toward the mini-van, store customers pushing loaded shopping carts steered clear. She could only hope that if the van belonged to the pet-nappers and they came back while she was casing it, they wouldn't want to tangle with the huge white dog, either.

Coming at the van from the front left side, Robyn's heart leaped into her throat when a Yorkshire terrier suddenly appeared in the side window, yapping with a frenzied fury that almost equaled Tawney's.

"What are you doing to my dog?" a woman snapped.

"Uh—" Startled, Robyn spun around to see a thin elderly woman glaring at her. "The, uh— window's not cracked and—"

The Yorkie continued to yap hysterically.

"But the window on the other side is!" The woman huffed. "I wouldn't leave my Poopsie in the car without cracking a window. And it's not *that* hot today, anyway. So why don't you and that oversized mutt just toddle along and mind your own business!"

"Yes, ma'am." Easing back, Robyn skirted the

woman and circled around the cart-return. Although it didn't seem likely the old lady could be a pet-napper, Louis suspected that a third person may have made the ransom call. This woman was definitely menacing and Robyn couldn't be certain that Poopsie actually belonged to her. Doubling back as the woman began unloading her groceries into the middle seat, Robyn glanced at the right rear corner. The paint was fine.

"Git!" the woman snapped as she pushed her empty cart around the end of the van.

Robyn got.

"Any luck, Ray? Over." Sitting in a bus stop shelter to rest a minute, Louis released the "talk" button so the walkie-talkie would receive.

"Not—thing, Louis." Static hissed and sputtered from the speaker, breaking up Ray's transmission. "If there's—hundred—vans in—Valley, I—find. . . ."

Rising, Louis stepped into the open. That helped a little, but didn't completely eliminate the interference. "Say again. Over."

"We've been out here for hours and—only seen two—vans!" Ray sounded exasperated.

"—had orange flames—side and the other didn't have—side windows. Over."

"Same here, Ray." Louis sighed, his desperation mounting as the hours passed. Since they knew the pet-nappers had been operating in the area for almost a week, he had been sure somebody would run across them. He had seen three black vans: one transporting five little leaguers to a game, one with double back doors instead of a hatchback, and one that was so dented and rusted a little cracked and peeling paint would hardly have been noticeable. "Have you heard from anyone? Over."

"Robyn called—an hour ago, but I—barely heard her. She's coming—empty, too. Alex called her and—nothing—zip. Over."

"No word from Nicole? Over."

"Not a peep. Over."

Exhaling, Louis scanned the street. A dark green mini-van passed going north. A red one zoomed by in the southbound lane. "I'm gonna cut over to Eighth Street and start back. Looks like we may have to resort to Plan B. Over."

"Roger that. I've—money with me. Over and out."

Clipping the walkie-talkie to his belt, Louis hopped back on his bike and turned east. His dad had flatly refused to consider a loan, probably because he hadn't finished paying off the last one yet. Pleading that it was a matter of life and death hadn't helped because he hadn't been able to explain whose life was in danger and why. If he was going to sell some of his silver coins, he couldn't afford to waste any more time. The Main Street Exchange was the only rare coin shop in Paradise Valley and it closed at five o'clock.

Suddenly worried because no one had heard from Nicole, Louis unclipped his walkie-talkie and tried to call her.

"Louis to Nicole. Come in, Nicole. Over."

The only answer was static hiss. Either Nicole was out of range or her walkie-talkie wasn't working!

Discouraged and tired, Nicole almost didn't see the black mini-van at the corner gas station. It was the only vehicle parked by the pumps. Figuring it was just another dead end, like the six others she had spotted during the day, she turned into the station and casually pedaled by.

And almost took a header onto the pavement when she saw the spot on the right rear corner where the paint was cracked and peeled.

The bike wobbled as she fought to regain her balance and tried to decide what to do. She had found the van, but she was on the far side of town with no idea what had happened to everyone else. The one time she had tried to check in on the walkie-talkie, all she had gotten was static.

The station door slammed closed.

Nicole glanced back as a short, pudgy man with bright red hair exited, counting his change. He went straight to the pump by the van and lifted the nozzle.

Afraid that he might get suspicious of a teenage girl who was showing an extraordinary amount of interest in his fueling procedure, Nicole turned right at the end of the building, then left around the end of the dumpster. Leaving the bike, she edged up the back side of the large green refuse container to keep an eye on the van.

Pressing the "talk" button, Nicole spoke into the walkie-talkie with quiet intensity. "Louis! Louis! Are you there?"

All she heard in reply was static.

Figures, Nicole thought as she hit the device against her hand, hoping to jar it into working just once. Half the gadgets Big Lou Driscoll sold only worked half the time and then they rarely functioned up to expectations. This particular gadget was a total bust.

"Louis! Ray! Alex! Robyn! Anybody—"

"—not fair, Stevie! Over." A young girl's voice suddenly came through loud and clear.

Surprised, Nicole fumbled with the walkie-talkie looking for the volume control.

"Is, too! Besides, I'm not *in* the house. So there!"

Glancing at the van, Nicole breathed easier. The pet-napper's attention was glued to the dollar amount window on the pump so he wouldn't go over the prepaid price. Which he had probably paid in cash, Nicole deduced. The crooks wouldn't want to leave a paper trail.

"You'd better not be, Lizzie. And you gotta say 'over' when you're done! Over."

"Get off the line!" Nicole ordered in a low but strained voice. Then, when the bickering dialogue continued without interruption, she realized that the two kids couldn't hear her, either. She turned the walkie-talkie off as the pet-napper replaced the gas nozzle and turned to fasten his gas cap.

Scurrying to her bike, Nicole walked it to the air pump at the corner of the building and pretended to check the pressure in the front tire.

When the man got in the van, she eased onto the seat and waited until he pulled out to make sure she headed in the same direction. Then she pedaled as fast as she could to keep up.

And lost sight of the van before she reached the end of the first block.

CHAPTER 8

Taking off the heavy binoculars, Ray hung them on his handlebars and glanced at his watch. "It's ten after five already! So where's Louis?"

Collapsing in the shade of a large tree by the side of Dave's trailer, Robyn just shrugged and tried to catch her breath. She had gone home to get her bike after taking Falcon back to Mrs. Mallory and had just arrived herself.

"Maybe Louis found the van after I lost it and can't get through on those worthless walkie-talkies!" Frustrated, Nicole slumped against the tree trunk.

"I doubt it. *His* was working just fine." Ray

sighed. "The last thing he told me was that he was going to The Main Street Exchange, but that was almost two hours ago."

"Maybe the coin shop is swamped with customers this afternoon." Pouring water into the small dish for Dusty, Alex set it down, then pulled out another dog biscuit. She had stopped to get her bike, too, and the dog had had to run to keep up on the way over to Dave's from her house. "I mean, it's the only place in town where Louis can sell his coins in a hurry to get the ransom money. So if the store's really busy, he wouldn't have any choice except to wait, right?"

"I suppose." Stretching out on the ground, Ray sighed again. "I just hope he gets back before those guys call."

"We've still got twenty minutes," Nicole said. "I'm sure it's not a problem."

"Actually," Louis said as he made his way down the hill toward them. "We've got a *big* problem."

Everyone just stared at him.

"The Main Street Exchange closes at *four* on Saturdays—not five." Louis hung his head. "So I don't have the ransom money because I didn't sell my coins."

"Oops." Ray sighed.

"If we don't have the ransom, then what's going to happen to Oscar?" Robyn closed her eyes, as though the thought was too terrible to contemplate.

"Before we panic, let's count our money and see how much we *do* have." Staying calm was not nearly as difficult for Alex. No one else was aware of Plan C. But she couldn't implement *her* plan unless Plan B went forward on schedule.

"Okay, but let's do it inside." Louis turned and headed toward the door. "I don't want to miss the pet-nappers when they call to give me instructions."

Huddling around the table inside Dave's trailer a few minutes later, everyone watched expectantly as Louis counted the money they had tossed into a pile.

"Well?" Ray leaned forward.

Louis sat back. "We're a little short."

"Like—how short?" Robyn asked.

Louis winced. "We've only got two hundred and sixteen dollars and fifty-three cents."

"That's not even *half!*" Nicole frowned.

"Maybe the pet-nappers will take it as a down-payment," Ray suggested.

"And let me pay off the rest on the installment

plan?" Rolling his eyes, Louis stood up and began to pace.

"Yeah, guess not." Ray sighed. "So now what do we do?"

Alex glanced down at the dog dozing at her feet. She had rescued Dusty from the thieves. There was no reason to think she couldn't rescue Oscar, too.

"Actually," Alex said, "we should go ahead as though we've got all the money."

Ray looked at her sharply.

"That won't work, Alex," Louis said. "I'm sure they'll count it before they let Oscar go."

"I'm sure they will, but it'll take them a couple of minutes to do it." Alex hesitated. She couldn't explain that she was going to turn herself into a puddle to enter the van and release the chimp, but she needed everyone's cooperation. Her gaze flicked to Ray. "A *lot* can happen in a couple of minutes."

Ray blinked, then frowned, then started as he suddenly realized she was planning to use her powers but couldn't come right out and say so. He instantly threw his support behind her.

"Alex is right, Louis. For one thing, we'd, uh— have a second chance to follow the van back to their hideout!"

"That's true," Nicole said cautiously. "Except they can drive a lot faster than we can pedal."

"We've still got to try. The thing is," Robyn reminded them, "Oscar may be our priority, but the pet-nappers have Baron and Ticket and who knows how many other pets stashed away somewhere, too."

"So we have to find out where," Ray said. "Once we know, we *can* call the police."

Nicole nodded. "Then *they* can raid the hideout and rescue everyone."

"That's right! The pet-nappers won't have time to 'dispose' of the animals if the police take them by surprise." Robyn brightened with hope.

"I won't argue with that, but we rescue Oscar first. *Before* we call the police," Louis said firmly. "I don't want him impounded as evidence or anything. And since we don't *have* the ransom money, we've got to assume that the pet-nappers won't just hand him over."

"So following the van is still our only hope?" Robyn slumped with a defeated sigh.

"Apparently," Nicole said grimly. "Which means we're in trouble."

"Not necessarily," Alex interjected. She was in total agreement with Louis about keeping Oscar out of police custody. Just for different reasons.

If the chimp zapped a law enforcement officer, word would get back to Danielle. The CEO of Paradise Valley Chemical had contacts in every branch of the city government, including the Police Department, and she could claim Oscar was a plant research animal.

"I can sneak into the van and get Oscar out before the pet-nappers know what's happening," Alex said enthusiastically. "Especially if you keep them distracted, Louis."

"No way, Alex!" Louis held up his hands and shook his head. "It's too dangerous. It's *my* fault Oscar got out so those guys could grab him in the first place. *I'll* sneak into the van."

"No!" Realizing he had reacted a little too strongly, Ray immediately covered himself. "You've got to pretend to be Dave making the payoff, Louis. Believe me. Alex is the best person for the job."

Although he obviously didn't like the idea of endangering someone else because he felt responsible for Oscar's capture, Louis had no choice but to give in.

"That's fine for Oscar," Robyn said, "but it won't help us find the other pets."

Alex had already considered that. "Up close, the dirt on the license plate won't totally hide the numbers because they're raised. Louis will be close enough to read it."

"Besides," Ray added, "we can still track the van back to the—"

The phone rang.

Dusty instantly jumped up to answer it.

Louis put his hand over the receiver so he couldn't.

"Tell them you've got the money, Louis." Alex met his uncertain gaze with a look of total confidence. "Trust me."

Nodding, Louis picked up the phone.

Since Robyn and Nicole had the fastest bikes, they hid in the brush where the quarry drive entered County Route 12. Equipped with one of the working walkie-talkies, the two girls would follow the van when it left the quarry whether Oscar had been rescued or not. They had a slim but fighting chance of succeeding because the old county road was riddled with potholes and curved a lot before it cut through the north end of town. Then the van would be slowed down by stop signs, traffic lights, and a thirty-mile-per-hour speed limit, all of which the pet-nappers had to obey if they didn't want to get stopped for a traffic violation. Aside from getting the chimp home safely, everyone was committed to saving the other pets and stopping the pet-nappers from ever stealing another animal.

Alex, Dusty, Ray, and Louis went through the chain-link gate, which was open just as the caller had told them it would be, and headed down the dirt road into the quarry. As Alex pedaled past large, silent earth-movers, empty dump trucks, and tall mounds of dirt and gravel, she had to admit the pet-nappers had picked the perfect spot for the exchange. Isolated on the edge of Paradise Valley, but only a fifteen-minute bike ride from Dave's trailer, the quarry was closed and no one was around. Although she had morphed to sneak in and out of the chemical plant and other risky places more times than she could count, the creepy quiet of the stone quarry played on her taut nerves. Maybe because she had never been in a situation in which so many innocent lives depended on her.

Running along beside her, even Dusty seemed tense and more alert than usual.

Stopping behind the base of the huge hopper that classified the rocks into different sizes, Louis peered over a supporting strut. The clearing by the quarry office was deserted. "Good. They're not here yet."

"But they will be soon." Ray checked the walkie-talkie clipped to his belt to make sure it was secure. "We'd better get into position."

Taking a deep breath, Louis nodded and slipped his walkie-talkie into a canvas bag strapped to his handlebars. If the thieves saw it, they might suspect a relay surveillance team was planning to track them.

Dusty looked at Alex expectantly, but she didn't have one of the com-devices. Only three of the walkie-talkies worked with any degree of reliability and the chase team needed them. Besides, after hearing Nicole's story about the two kids breaking in on the same frequency, Louis had insisted that they couldn't take a chance someone somewhere would talk and expose her while she was inside the van. He didn't know that both she and the walkie-talkie would be morphed into a liquid state. And since her own voice could be heard when she was morphed, she didn't know if a transmitted voice would be audible or not.

"Ready, Alex?" Ray asked.

"Let's go." Pedaling as fast as she could, Alex reached the back of the office shack in seconds and parked her bike.

Ray stayed mounted. "Are you sure you're going to be all right?"

"Yes, Ray. I've done this a lot, remember?" Alex smiled, hoping to convey more confidence than she felt. "Robyn and Nicole will have a better chance of keeping up with the van if they have some idea where it's going."

"Let's hope so." Raising the binoculars to his eyes, Ray looked up toward the ridge on the north side of the quarry. From there, he would be able to see the two-lane county road for a couple of miles in both directions and could guide the girls through the walkie-talkies.

"So you'd better get moving." Slinging her backpack strap over her handlebars, Alex waited until Ray disappeared behind a mountain of gray gravel, then edged around the side of the shack. Louis was in the clearing, pacing in small circles. Less than a minute later, the van drove in.

Leaving the engine running and the front doors open, both men got out. They were wearing full-face ski masks so Louis wouldn't be able to identify them, but they looked ridiculous. The tall man's nose obviously itched under the knit covering and he kept scratching at the cap.

"Stay, Dusty!" Alex ordered in a low but stern voice.

The collie whined in protest, but he sat.

Quickly morphing into a shimmering puddle, Alex skirted the base of the office. Spotting a tire rut that led almost directly to the open van door, she elongated and slid into it. Louis and the two men were too engrossed in the ransom transaction to notice the silvery ribbon gliding swiftly through the shallow channel.

The men stopped before Louis. The short one held out his hand. Neither of them spoke.

"Okay. Here's the money." Louis's voice cracked nervously as he slapped the bundle of bills into the man's hand. "Where's the chimp?"

While the plump man counted, the tall man put his hand on Louis's chest when he boldly tried to move toward the van.

Flowing out of the tire rut, Alex oozed up and into the front seat. She immediately spotted a cellular phone and a spiral notebook lying open on the floor and took a moment to glance at the notebook. The pages were filled with names, addresses, phone numbers, and dates, each with five-hundred-dollar notations, some of which were checked off.

Outside, Alex heard Louis raise his voice as

he tried to stall the two men. They had obviously figured out that their ransom pay-off was short by almost three hundred dollars!

"Look, it's all I could get on such short notice. If you'd just give me more time—wait!" A distinct note of panic suddenly infected Louis's voice. "Where're you going?"

With time running out, Alex glided over the front seat and into the back of the van. She pooled in an abrupt, stunned, and shimmering halt.

The cages were empty!

"I'm sure we can work something out!" Louis shouted. "What's the rush? Come on, guys! Let's talk!"

Both men jumped into the front seat and the van lurched forward as they slammed their doors closed.

Sloshing against the side of the van as it careened around a curve, Alex struggled into a plastic storage pocket molded into the wheel-well and forced herself to stay calm. Even though she could stay morphed for increasingly longer periods of time than when she had first acquired her powers, she couldn't stay morphed indefinitely.

But that wasn't the worst of her problems.

"I think that kid's up to something, Dan." Ripping off his ski mask, the tall, thin driver scratched the whisker stubble on his face.

"Yep." Peeling off his ski mask, short, stout Dan ran his fingers through shocking red hair. "We've been on borrowed time ever since those two girls made us lose that cat the other day. Maybe it's time to get out of this town, Burt."

Still scratching, Burt nodded and sighed. "Agreed."

"After we get the other ransoms, right?"

"Don't think so, Dan. We can't spend a cent in jail." Burt grunted as the van hit a pothole. "We'll ditch the animals and then we're out of here—tonight."

Alex stifled a gurgling gasp.

How were they planning to "ditch" the animals?

Alex shuddered, dreading the answer, and knowing she'd find out before long. An accidental passenger, she was speeding toward the pet-nappers' hideout.

But—if Nicole and Robyn lost track of the van, she had no way of contacting anyone for help when she got there!

CHAPTER 9

From the ridge, Ray watched the events unfold through his father's high-powered binoculars and gave Robyn and Nicole a play-by-play description through the walkie-talkie. The girls had moved onto the road so it would look like they were just riding by when the van left the quarry. Everything was going according to plan—until the two masked men suddenly whirled and ran to get back into the van.

"Uh-oh. They're gonna take off! Over."

"Where's Alex? What about Oscar?" Nicole asked, then added the standard "over" so Ray would know she was finished.

"I think she's still in the van!" Ray increased

the magnification on the binoculars to scan the area, but he didn't see any silvery puddles. Then the van suddenly started moving. "Get ready! They're leaving and they're leaving fast! Over."

Louis turned and dashed for his bike.

"They're leaving now? With Alex trapped in the back?" Robyn squealed. "Huh? Oh, uh— over!"

"Yeah." Numb, Ray stared at the empty clearing when the van sped off, but there were no patches of shimmering ooze anywhere. Alex hadn't had time to release the chimp and escape.

Retrieving his walkie-talkie from the canvas bag, Louis broke in. "Ray? Where are you? Where's Alex? Over!"

"I'm on the ridge—" Before Ray could finish, Dusty came charging across the dirt lot and snatched the walkie-talkie from Louis's hand as he lowered it. Then, with the device firmly gripped in his mouth, the dog took off at full speed after Alex and the van!

Stunned, Louis hesitated a moment, then jumped on his bike and raced after the dog.

Ray zeroed in on Robyn and Nicole as the van reached the end of the drive. Riding west toward town, the girls increased their speed as the van turned onto the highway and sped by them.

However, even though they were riding fast bikes and the van would be slowed down by potholes and curves, it was instantly clear that they wouldn't be able to keep up.

Scanning back to the dog, Ray suddenly had a farfetched idea. The county road curved back toward the quarry before it turned west again, and Dusty could make great time going cross-country—if he could get the dog headed in the right direction. Louis's walkie-talkie had been turned on when Dusty grabbed it and a button only had to be pushed to *talk*—not to receive.

"Dusty! Go to the right! Go right!"

Falling way behind Nicole and the van, Robyn slowed down as Louis turned onto the highway. "What was that, Ray? Over."

Ray didn't respond immediately. He watched as the dog faltered and veered to the left. "No! To the right! Go right!" The instant the dog turned to the right, Ray urged him on. "Yes! Go, go, go! Find Alex!"

Flying through the tall grass and leaping over clumps of brush, Dusty hit the highway seconds after the van passed. Nicole hadn't even entered the curve yet. Then, when the road curved to the left a little farther on, Dusty cut the corner across another field, shaving more seconds off the van's lead.

Catching up with Robyn, Louis looked toward the ridge as she asked for clarification. "What's going on, Ray? It sounds like you're talking to the dog. Over."

"Yeah! And it's working!" Ray said excitedly. Actually, when he stopped to think about it, Dusty's actions were perfectly logical. If he was a trained assistance dog like Nicole thought, he would know how to take simple directions. The real problem was whether or not he could maintain the grueling pace. If he didn't lose sight of the van and the pet-nappers' hideout wasn't too far away, there was a good chance the dog would make it.

"What's Dusty doing?" Robyn asked incredulously. "Over."

"He's taking the walkie-talkie to Alex!"

When the van finally jolted to a stop and Burt turned off the engine, Alex calculated that they had been driving for roughly ten minutes. Three or four of those minutes had been spent at stop signs and traffic lights. With luck, her friends weren't far behind. Unfortunately, the backup that might or might not be on its way would definitely *not* arrive in time to help her out of the immediate crisis. She had materialized to conserve her strength during the ride. Now she had to morph back into a liquid or risk getting caught by Burt and Dan.

"Let's not waste any time." Shoving the cell phone into his back pocket, Dan sighed. "I gotta real bad feeling."

"Yeah. Me, too," Burt said. "Nobody's gotten this close to catching us in five years. Ever since you figured out that since people were willing to pay rewards for lost pets, they'd probably be willing to pay ransoms for stolen ones."

"Yeah, well, these kids aren't going to catch us, either. We'll be over the state line and scouting another town in a couple of days. Another month and we can head home with enough cash to keep us going for months." Dan kicked his door open and got out.

"Yep." Jumping out on the driver's side, Burt slammed his door shut. As he stepped away, he was jerked back. Opening the door a crack, he pulled his shirttail free, then slammed it closed again.

Morphing just as Dan threw open the rear hatch, Alex oozed into the front seat. However, Dan didn't look inside the back of the van. He hurried away to catch up to Burt, who was unlocking the door of an old, abandoned gas station.

On the corner of Watson Drive and Forty-second Street!

Alex knew exactly where she was! However, although there was probably a pay phone somewhere on the block, her friends were scattered somewhere between here and the quarry and couldn't be reached by phone.

As soon as the men disappeared inside, Alex oozed into the back of the van, materialized, and scanned the street visible through the open hatch. None of her friends were in sight.

Except—Dusty!

Alex gasped in astonishment as the collie charged into view, leaped into the back of the van, and dropped a walkie-talkie into her hand. Picking it up, Alex gave the dog a quick hug. She was awed and thrilled by his unexpected and heroic appearance, but too pressed for time to dwell on it.

"Come on, boy. We gotta get out of here before those guys come back!"

One of the large garage bay doors began to rattle open.

Dusty was right behind her as Alex jumped

out and scurried for cover around the corner of the building. Gesturing at the dog to stay back, Alex flattened herself against the wall. She didn't know whose idea it had been to send him after her with the walkie-talkie, but it was brilliant. Almost as brilliant as Dusty's uncanny determination to deliver it!

Depressing the "talk" button, Alex whispered into the transmitter. "Ray! Can you hear me? It's Alex! Over."

Nervously nibbling her lip, Alex waited for a response. There wasn't any. She knew the unit worked because they had tested the three good ones before they had gotten to the quarry. Wondering if the old building was blocking the signal, Alex turned the device off and clipped it to the waistband of her jeans. She wouldn't stay hidden long if someone shouted through it within Dan and Burt's hearing.

Peeking around the edge of the building, Alex frowned as the two men hurried toward the back of the van. Both of them were lugging animal carriers.

"It shouldn't take longer than half an hour to load up." Grunting, Dan heaved his carrier into the back of the van. A small dog yelped.

"Then another forty minutes to get out to

Sandstone Gulch. We don't want anyone watching when we turn these animals loose." Setting his carrier into the van, Burt paused to wipe his brow. "After that, we'll be home free and long gone."

Alex gritted her teeth in total fury. Sandstone Gulch was a rugged desert area with no water. Any domestic animal dumped there would die of thirst or starve before it found its way back to civilization. If the coyotes didn't get it first!

"Not in *my* lifetime!" Alex muttered. Motioning for Dusty to stay and be quiet, she eased toward the back of the building to look for another way inside. She found a boarded-up window.

Fortified by anger and a few minutes rest, Alex quickly morphed and slithered through a split in the plywood. Halfway through, she paused just long enough to familiarize herself with the layout. A dozen small- to medium-sized carriers holding cats and small dogs were stacked on a center table. Half-a-dozen larger carriers and wire cages stood on the floor right below her, but she couldn't see inside them. Since the lights weren't on, she assumed the electricity in the abandoned station wasn't hooked up. The daylight coming in through the large open front door was dim, leaving most of the rear section bathed in dark shadow.

Burt and Dan walked in, then stopped to get cold sodas out of a cooler sitting beside a pile of old tires. Dan set the cellular phone on a shelf by the door.

Gliding to the floor, Alex oozed around the base of several large cases. A large dog with short, curly hair that she thought might be Baron whined as she slid by. Oscar was slumped in the corner of a big wire cage looking totally bummed-out. However, as she oozed inside, he began to screech with excited joy.

"Must be time to tranquilize the chimp again." Dan sighed.

"Must be." Burt pulled a banana and a small box out of the cooler. "It's your turn, Dan."

"No, it's not! I fed him this morning, Burt."

"No, you didn't," Burt insisted.

"Shhhhh!" Alex gurgled. "Come on, boy! It's puddle time!"

Taking the hint, Oscar stopped screeching and morphed ever so slowly. Then he followed as Alex zipped out of the cage into the dark shadows along the side wall.

"Forget it, Burt. He shut up."

Noticing that the liquid Oscar was moving

more sluggishly than normal, too, Alex realized that the tranquilizer was still inhibiting the chimp's ability to use his powers. Certain that the pet-nappers wouldn't recognize the silvery puddle as the missing chimp, she left Oscar and materialized behind a cardboard box that was half-full of empty oil cans.

Then she waited and watched. Although the two men collected money from heartbroken people who wanted their pets back and were planning to dump their hostages in the desert, Dan and Burt didn't seem too dangerous. She didn't want to hurt them, but she had to make sure they didn't carry out their escape plan.

Squashing his empty soda can, Dan heaved it into a corner.

Alex telekinetically grabbed it and threw it back.

Yelping with surprise, Dan ducked. The crumpled can bounced off his shoulder.

"What?" Burt asked impatiently, his hand hovering above another carrier.

"That soda can just attacked me!"

Burt scowled. "No, it didn't."

"Yes, it did."

Reaching into the cardboard box with her mind, Alex picked up several empty oil cans.

Aiming high to avoid hitting the men, she telekinetically heaved them across the garage so that they hit the far wall and clattered to the floor. Dan and Burt both yelped and threw their arms over their heads.

"I'm outta here!" Dan turned to bolt out the front door.

"Wait! Somebody must be in here!" Straightening up, Burt turned in a frantic circle.

Telekinetically grabbing half-a-dozen of the fallen oil cans, Alex sent them rolling back toward Burt. He jumped at the sound and gasped as the cans rolled to a complete stop in a straight line in front of him. When he backed up a step, the cans followed, then stopped when he stopped.

"Maybe you're right, Dan," Burt said nervously. "Let's get out of here." Stumbling over his own feet, Burt lunged toward the door behind Dan—

—just as Dusty appeared in the large opening, his lip curled in a menacing snarl.

Confronted with the intimidating, snarling dog, both men hesitated, buying Alex a few seconds to execute her next move. Tugging with all her telekinetic might, she toppled the pile of old tires. Several of them bounced and rolled between the door and the men, forcing Dan and Burt back. Then, letting fly with a long-range zapper, she triggered the garage door closed.

Barking, Dusty dashed inside before the massive door hit concrete.

Incited by the collie, all the other captive dogs began to bark.

Oscar squealed with amused chimp laughter from the shadows, then scrambled across the floor to join the dog.

"How'd he get out, Burt?"

"I don't know, Dan. Maybe you didn't lock the cage after you gave him his banana this morning."

"Yes, I did!"

Alex sent another zapper into the wiring and the lights flashed on, abruptly ending Dan and Burt's argument.

Confused and terrified, the men cautiously eased back as Dusty and Oscar slowly advanced.

Realizing that the pet-nappers were headed for two large empty cages on the floor by the back wall, Alex telekinetically removed the open padlocks, released the latches, and opened the doors. When Oscar started jumping up and down and screeching, Dan and Burt each dove into the safety of a cage. Pulling the doors closed behind them, they ducked and buried their heads in their arms as the dog and chimp charged.

Neither one of them saw the padlocks float off the floor, slip through the latch holes, and lock.

Sagging with relief, Alex smiled as Dusty sat down to silently guard the captives. He didn't even flinch when Oscar waddled over and awkwardly patted him on the head.

However, Alex couldn't afford to let the two men see her in the garage. Too many inexplicable things had happened, and as things stood now, they didn't have a clue why. Waving Dusty over, she draped an arm around him and held out her hand to Oscar. As soon as she had the chimp's attention, she doused the lights and morphed. Not wanting to be left behind, the chimp dissolved into a silvery puddle and followed her through the open door into the waning light outside.

Using the front of the van for cover, Alex materialized herself and the dog. Totally unperturbed by the transformation, Dusty yawned and stretched out on the pavement. Oscar, however, remained liquefied and began zooming back and forth across the parking area for the sheer joy of being morphed and free.

Unclipping the walkie-talkie, Alex turned it

back on and pressed the "talk" button. "Hello? Ray? Louis? Anybody out there? Over."

"Alex!" Ray's anxious voice sputtered through the speaker. "Where are you? Over."

"That old gas station on Watson. Over."

"Really? I'm only a block away! Be right there. Over."

Louis came on the instant Ray signed off. "What about Oscar? Is he okay? Over."

Alex glanced at the jet-propelled puddle and grinned as the liquid chimp slid to a stop and suddenly morphed back into solid form. "He's fine. But you'd better get over here soon or you won't make it back to Dave's before Dave does! Over!"

"We're on our way! O—"

"Wait!" Robyn interrupted. "What happened to those guys? And the animals? Over."

"The animals are fine." Alex looked at the closed bay door and grinned with intense satisfaction. "And those guys aren't going anywhere until their police escort arrives."

Signing off, Alex laughed as a totally pooped Oscar flopped down by Dusty. The dog glanced back as the chimp nestled against his side, then lowered his muzzle onto his front paws in the dog version of a resigned sigh.

"Now comes the *really* hard part."

With a resigned sigh of her own, Alex opened the van door and picked up the notebook that was still on the floor. Since putting off the inevitable wouldn't make it any easier, she slid into the front seat and flipped back a page to the entries for Thursday. Alex couldn't hold back the tears as she read the scrawled handwriting.

Miriam Turner/ Jefferson Road/ male collie/ escaped.

The ransom call had been made anyway.

CHAPTER 10

Using a stubby pencil she found in the glove compartment, Alex finished jotting down Miriam Turner's phone number just as Ray, Robyn, Nicole, and Louis rode into the old station. Tucking the paper into her jeans pocket, she slid out of the front seat with the notebook.

"Ticket!" Bursting into joyous laughter, Robyn dropped her mom's bike and raced to the back of the van. Quickly opening one of the carriers, she pulled out a small, squirming white poodle who was just as deliriously happy to see her. Hugging Ticket to her chest, Robyn looked at Alex with a questioning frown. "What about Baron?"

"I saw a dog that fits his description inside. He's not happy, but he seems to be okay."

"Had a tough day, huh, Oscar?" Peering down at the dozing chimp, Louis shook his head. "Probably not as tough as mine was, though."

Awakening suddenly, Oscar leaped into Louis's arms, almost knocking him over. His lips folded back in a huge chimp grin of amused delight.

"Come on. We gotta get going." With the chimp riding piggyback, Louis hopped onto his bike and called to Alex. "Do me a favor, okay? Not a word about any of this to Dave—ever!"

"Not a word," Alex promised. She wasn't going to talk to Dave about anything ever unless she absolutely had to. As Louis and Oscar raced off, Dusty trotted over and slipped his muzzle into her hand. She choked back another rush of emotion as Ray and Nicole joined her.

"You are one smart dog, Dusty." Kneeling down, Ray vigorously rubbed the dog behind the ears. "If I hadn't seen it with my own eyes, I wouldn't have believed it."

Smiling sadly, Alex nodded. "I have to say, I was shocked when I saw him racing to my rescue! Then again, he *does* have this thing about phones."

"Where are the pet-nappers, Alex?" Nicole asked.

"Locked up in dog kennels."

"How'd you manage that?"

Ray looked at her pointedly. He knew she had probably used her powers, but Nicole didn't.

"Uh—" Alex blinked at Nicole, then decided that an explanation containing an essence of the truth would probably work without raising any suspicions. "Well, I snuck in and let Oscar out and then this box with a bunch of empty cans fell off a shelf and they crashed all over the place. So when Oscar and Dusty cornered them, Burt and Dan were so upset and confused, they got into the dog kennels to get away. I guess Oscar put the padlocks on and locked them because I stayed hidden and they didn't see *me* at all. I, uh—really don't want the police to know I had anything to do with their capture, okay?"

"Gotcha." Ray nodded and winked.

"But what if the District Attorney needs your testimony to put those guys away?" Nicole asked, alarmed.

Alex handed her the spiral notebook. "This should satisfy the District Attorney. It has all the information you'll need to locate the animals' owners, too. And there's a cellular phone on a shelf by the door you can use to call the police."

"What are you going to do?" Nicole's eyes

widened as she thumbed through the notebook that proved Burt and Dan had been moving from town to town, stealing pets, and collecting ransoms for a long time. It was all the evidence needed to convict the two men.

"I've got Dusty's owner's phone number." Struggling to maintain her composure, Alex shrugged. "But I think I'll take him home and call from there."

Leaving her friends to handle things with the police at the garage, Alex set out on the long walk home. Ray had volunteered to get her bike and backpack from the quarry and she had gratefully agreed. She didn't want to worry about anything right now. She just wanted to spend this one last walk alone with Dusty to say good-bye.

Sensing her sadness without knowing why she was sad, Dusty hugged Alex's side the whole way home. Walking with her hand on his soft, furry back, Alex couldn't avoid facing the feeling of loneliness that became more profound with each step. Dusty had made his own special place in her heart and when he was gone, she knew that nothing would ever fill up that particular empty space again.

By the time Alex turned onto her street, she

had accepted the fact that Dusty belonged to someone else. However, she was surprised to see an unfamiliar car parked in the driveway. And even more surprised when her father, who must have been watching for her through the front window, rushed outside.

"Alex! Where have you been?"

"Sorry. Guess it is kinda late—" Alex stopped talking as Dusty suddenly bolted for the front door.

"I'm afraid I've got some bad news—or good news. Depends on how you look at it, I guess." Putting his arm around her shoulders, Mr. Mack walked Alex to the door where Dusty was frantically pawing to get in.

Alex didn't need an explanation. "Miriam Turner's here to get Dusty, isn't she, Dad?"

"Yes, but how did you know—"

Alex handed him the slip of notebook paper with the woman's name and phone number. "It's a long story, but I'd like to save it for later, okay?"

"Sure." Squeezing Alex's shoulder, Mr. Mack opened the door.

Dusty dashed into the house.

Stepping inside, Alex paused as the dog spun in excited circles for a minute, then sat down and put his head in an elderly woman's lap. Tears welled up in the woman's eyes as she leaned over and kissed him soundly on the head.

Mrs. Mack was sitting on the sofa beside another elderly woman.

"Dusty, Dusty. . . ."

As Alex watched, any lingering reservations she had about returning Dusty vanished. Now she understood those wistful looks of longing she had seen in his soft brown eyes. Dusty liked her a lot, but Miriam Turner was the absolute center of his universe.

"I was so sure I'd never see you again, especially after that nasty man called—" The woman looked up. "Oh, my. Listen to me babbling on and on. You must be Alex!"

"Right," Mr. Mack said. "Alex, this is Mrs. Turner."

"Her friend and neighbor, Mrs. Gross—" Mrs. Mack smiled at the woman beside her. "—spotted one of your signs and drove Mrs. Turner right over.

"Would you believe that someone *stole* Dusty and then had the nerve to call and ask for a ransom even though he had escaped?" Mr. Mack shook his head in disgust.

"Yeah, Dad. I would." Smiling, Alex walked

forward to shake Mrs. Turner's hand. Then she noticed the cane leaning against the chair.

"I've been totally frantic," Mrs. Turner said. "Five hundred dollars is a lot of money for someone living on a fixed income."

"But we would have paid it," Mrs. Gross said firmly. "All our friends chipped in and we only had fifty dollars left to go. I'm glad things worked out differently, but I sure hope those horrible men get caught and punished."

"You know," Alex said casually, "I heard that the police broke up a pet-napping ring just this afternoon!"

"Really?" Mrs. Mack raised a questioning eyebrow.

Alex ignored it—for the moment.

"Well, I certainly hope so." Mrs. Turner nodded emphatically. "You see, Alex, Dusty's not only one of my two best friends in the whole world, I wouldn't be able to live on my own without him. I have trouble walking and he does a lot of it for me."

"He's a trained assistance dog, isn't he?" Hoping she wasn't overstepping her bounds, Alex petted Dusty's head.

"Yes, he is." Mrs. Turner cocked her head thoughtfully. "Your mother tells me that you and Dusty got along splendidly and that you took extremely good care of him, too."

"In fact, Alex," Mrs. Mack said, "you've done such a good job with Dusty, your father and I don't see any reason why you shouldn't have a dog of your own."

"Even if the allergy medicine *doesn't* keep working," Mr. Mack added.

Surprised and pleased, Alex smiled. "Thanks. I'll remember that—if I ever find the *right* dog. The right dog for me, that is."

"I see." Mrs. Mack glanced at Mr. Mack and shrugged.

Alex didn't know how to explain it. It meant a lot that her mom and dad felt she was responsible enough to take care of a pet. But Robyn had been absolutely right about the intangible and unbreakable bond that instantly sprang into being when a person met *the* dog. There was no doubt that Dusty was the right dog for Mrs. Turner. And, Alex thought wistfully, he was also a really tough act to follow.

"Well, in that case, Alex—" Mrs. Turner hesitated. "Could I impose on you for another favor?"

"Sure. Name it."

"Would you mind coming over a couple of

times a week to take Dusty out for a walk? Or maybe even a romp in the park! If there's one thing I can't do, it's romp, and he could really use the exercise!"

"No problem! I'd love to."

"On one condition," Mr. Mack said firmly, but with a twinkle in his eye. "You have to bring him here to visit every once in a while. In fact, why don't you all come over tomorrow?! I just got a new gas grill and—"

The phone rang.

As Mr. Mack took a step forward, Mrs. Mack stopped him with a casual wave of her hand "Don't bother, George. The dog will get it."

Everyone laughed as Dusty bounded for the kitchen.

One thing was certain, Alex thought as she studied her parents' amused faces. If and when she ever *did* find the right dog, he would absolutely have to learn to answer the phone!

About the Author

Diana G. Gallagher lives in Minnesota with her husband, Marty Burke, three dogs, three cats, and a cranky parrot. When she's not writing, she likes to read, walk the dogs, and look for cool stuff at garage sales for her grandsons, Jonathon and Alan.

Diana and Marty are musicians who perform traditional and original Irish and American folk music at coffeehouses and conventions around the country. Marty sings and plays the twelve-string guitar and banjo. In addition to singing backup harmonies, Diana plays rhythm guitar and a round, Celtic drum called a *bodhran*.

A Hugo Award–winning artist, Diana is best known for her series *Woof: The House Dragon*. Her first adult novel, *The Alien Dark*, appeared in 1990. She and Marty coauthored *The Chance Factor*, a STARFLEET ACADEMY VOYAGER book. In addition to other STAR TREK novels for intermediate readers, Diana has written many books in other series published by Minstrel Books, including *The Secret World of Alex Mack*, *Are You Afraid of the Dark?*, and *The Mystery Files of Shelby Woo*. She is currently working on original young adult novels for the Archway Paperback series *Sabrina, the Teenage Witch*.

NICKELODEON/MINSTREL BOOKS POINTS PROGRAM

Official Rules

1. **HOW TO COLLECT POINTS**: Points may be collected by purchasing books in the following series, *The Secret World of Alex Mack*™, *Are You Afraid of the Dark?*™, and *The Mystery Files of Shelby Woo*™. Only books in the series published March 1998 and after are eligible for program. Points can be redeemed for merchandise by completing the coupons (found in the back of the books) and mailing with a check or money order in the exact amount to cover postage and handling to Nickelodeon/Minstrel Points Program, P.O. Box 7777-G140, Mt. Prospect, IL 60056-7777. Each coupon is worth 5 points. Copies of coupons are not valid. Simon & Schuster is not responsible for lost, late, illegible, incomplete, stolen, postage-due, or misdirected mail.

2. **40 POINT MINIMUM**: Each redemption request must contain a minimum of 40 points, or 8 coupons, in order to redeem for merchandise. Limit one merchandise request per envelope: 8 coupons (40 points), 12 coupons (60 points), 15 coupons (75 points), or 20 coupons (100 points).

3. **ELIGIBILITY**: Open to legal residents of the United States (excluding Puerto Rico) and Canada (excluding Quebec) only. Void where taxed, licensed, restricted, or prohibited by law. Redemption requests from groups, clubs, or organizations will not be honored.

4. **DELIVERY**: Allow 6-8 weeks for delivery of merchandise.

5. **MERCHANDISE**: All merchandise is subject to availability and may be replaced with an item of merchandise of equal or greater value at the sole discretion of Simon & Schuster.

6. **ORDER DEADLINE**: All redemption requests must be received by January 31, 1999, or while supplies last. Offer may not be combined with any other promotional offer from Simon & Schuster. Employees and the immediate family members of such employees of Simon & Schuster, its parent company, subsidiaries, divisions and related companies and their respective agencies and agents are ineligible to participate.

COMPLETE THE COUPON AND MAIL TO
NICKELODEON/MINSTREL POINTS PROGRAM
P.O. BOX 7777-G140
MT. PROSPECT, IL 60056-7777

NAME_____

ADDRESS_____

CITY _____ STATE _____ ZIP _____

THIS COUPON WORTH FIVE POINTS
Offer expires January 31, 1999

I have enclosed __ coupons and a check/money order (in U.S. currency only) made payable to "Nickelodeon/Minstrel Books Points Program" to cover postage and handling.

❏ 8 coupons (+ $3.50 postage and handling)   ❏ 15 coupons (+ $3.50 postage and handling)

❏ 12 coupons (+ $3.50 postage and handling)   ❏ 20 coupons (+ $5.50 postage and handling)
1464(2of2)